ALTERNATE PURPOSE

CHRISTOPHER COATES

Prologue

YEAR 2000

THE LIGHT RAIN FELL, AND THE MOON WASN'T VISIBLE BECAUSE of the heavy cloud cover. The weather was one of the many reasons why they'd picked tonight for this mission. A long row of streetlights illuminated the sidewalk, and the usually busy road had minimal traffic at this time of night. The bright sign by the building read *North East Regional Hospital*. About a hundred yards south of the sign was a narrow paved drive. There, a smaller unlit sign read *Authorized Traffic Only*. This drive led to a dark alcove between the original hospital and an addition that was added on in the late '70s. This area was restricted and unlit because no one wanted to see where the hospital kept the dumpsters. There were several hedges and a few ornamental trees in place to help partially obscure the drive.

Without warning, deep in the alcove, a neon blue light began to form between two dumpsters. It started about three feet off the ground and quickly grew to about six-feet high and two-and-a-half-feet wide. As soon as it reached full size, a medium-height woman with a slender build stepped from the portal and into the alcove. The light disappeared. During the six seconds the portal existed, there was a connection between our time period and another, which wouldn't exist again for almost a hundred years.

The woman stumbled, grabbed hold of the dumpster, and used it to balance herself. She took several deep breaths to help her focus, and then withdrew a small device from the pocket of the light blue hospital scrubs she wore and pressed it to her neck. She grimaced from a brief moment of pain where she had touched her neck. Then she relaxed as a warm feeling passed through her body. She returned the advanced auto-injector to her pocket and waited for a few seconds as the four medications took effect. She could already feel that the analgesic and powerful stimulant were working, and she started walking toward the sidewalk. The anti-nausea drug seemed to be helping, but not nearly as well. The fourth medication she couldn't detect, but she was told that it would slow down the lethal cellular collapse that was destroying her body.

She knew she had to get moving. The auto-injector held only two more doses and she needed to accomplish her mission before the final one wore off. She exited the alcove and moved to the sidewalk. Turning right, she strode toward the main hospital entrance with growing concern as she advanced. Her nausea seemed to be getting worse with each step and she could already feel her strength fading. Fortunately, she knew the layout of the hospital, having studied it well before her mission. The main entrance was just ahead and only a few other people were heading in the same direction she was.

The woman passed through the glass sliding door, and a security guard sat at a desk just inside. She turned the ID tag that hung from her scrubs so the guard could see the North East Region logo, and kept walking. The ID bore the name Abby Russell. That had been a joke by those that had fabricated the card. Abby Russell was the name of the last person to ever serve as President of the United States.

"Thanks. Have a good shift," the guard said.

The dying woman continued to walk, thinking how easy that had been. She knew the minimal levels of security were a primary reason for using this time period for the mission. She made her way to the bank of elevators, double checking her knowledge against the sign, which said that Maternity was on the fourth floor. Once the elevator door closed, she leaned back against the wall as the car started to move. She closed her eyes, resting, and thankful that she was alone. The pain continued to increase. Her head hurt the worst, but her gut and extremities also ached and that pain was getting worse rapidly.

The elevator doors opened, and with considerable effort, she forced herself to walk out of the elevator car and down the hall. She knew she wasn't walking straight and even felt herself stumbling, but she needed to keep going. She hoped no one would see her and think she was intoxicated. Per the plan, it was still too early for another injection. If she took them too soon, she wouldn't be able to make it back to the portal and home.

Casually she passed the nurses station, noting one man seated working on a computer. She smiled, relieved to see that the research had been correct and her scrubs matched his. At least her dress wouldn't draw attention.

Next, down the hall was the infant room. Inside were twelve bassinettes, only six of which had babies in them. A female nurse was in there, changing the diaper on one of the infants. Neither of the staff had paid any attention to the stranger, who purposefully traversed the corridor. At the end of the hall, she turned left and found what she was looking for—a door marked *Utility*. She struggled but managed to open the door, her dexterity failing, then stepped inside and let it close behind her. After removing the auto-injector from her pocket, she again pressed it to the side of her neck. The warm feeling returned, and so did her strength and alertness. The pain was somewhat diminished but still significant.

The room contained bins for dirty linens, and partially full trash cans as well as cleaning supplies. She moved to the utility sink and inserted the stopper, and took two sealed packets from her pocket, ripped them open and dumped the powdered contents into the sink. She raised the top to her scrubs, took from her belt two small bottles that she had attached on either side. Each was about eight ounces. She unscrewed the caps, took a deep breath and poured the green liquid over the powder. The effect was immediate. Harmless white chemical smoke began filling the utility closet. She turned and left the room, making sure to leave the door ajar to allow the pungent chemical smoke to fill the hall. She headed back toward the room with the newborns. Just before getting there, she stepped into an unoccupied patient room. She moved into the shadows and waited. After two full minutes, her anxiety started to grow. The waiting was taking much too long. The pain was back, almost as bad as right before her last dosage, and her thinking was getting fuzzy.

Eventually, she could smell the smoke as it worked up the hall. She heard concerned voices approaching and watched the woman and then the man hurry past her hiding spot, heading for the source of the smoke. As soon as it seemed safe, she stepped out of the room, looking left and right, then crossed over to the nursery, where she removed from her belt a device the size of a deck of playing cards and held it at the card reader. The door buzzed open. Defeating the primitive electronic security had been one of the simplest parts of the mission.

She stepped in and read the names on the bassinets, looking for Devin Baker. The first name she saw belonged to a cute infant girl named Tasha Doller. She recognized this name. Tasha had been the subject of an earlier mission. Unfortunately, Tasha died in a drowning accident in her early teens, before she could ever be of use. Devin was next to Tasha and he was sleeping peacefully. The trespasser quickly unwrapped him, removed a new single dose auto-injector from her other pocket, and pressed it to his leg. As rapidly as her shaking hands would allow, she re-wrapped the now-crying infant and left the room. She stepped out and strode to the elevator, slipping the expended auto-injector in her pocket. The elevator arrived and she got in and injected herself for the third time and final time. With this injection, the improvement was minimal.

As she exited the elevator, she removed two slips of paper from her pocket. One said *succeeded*, and the other, *failed*. She crumpled up the one that indicated failure and threw it in a trash can she passed and returned the other to her pocket. The planners had known that she wouldn't be in any condition to write a note at this point in the suicide mission.

She approached the exit with almost no strength left and was close to vomiting. Out of the corner of her eye, she could see the guard watching her as she walked. No doubt he could tell she wasn't feeling well.

"Going home already?"

She gave him a weak smile. "I'm not sure what I came down with, but it hit me fast."

"Well, I hope you're feeling better."

Rather than answer, she gave him a slight wave. She exited, the crisp night air feeling good. She made it to the sidewalk before she vomited. She could see and taste the blood. Her stomach felt a little better and she tried to increase her pace, but her coordination was failing and she tripped and landed face down on the sidewalk. With extreme effort, she used a light pole for balance and managed to make it back to her feet and continued toward the drive that led to the dumpsters.

Feeling something like a tear on her cheek, she wiped it away and noticed it was blood. Bleeding from the eyes and nose were possibilities she knew about. She entered the alcove, keeping one hand on the wall of the old building to help steady her balance, and struggled along. After making it to the dumpster, she leaned her back against it and removed from her pocket the last item she was carrying. It was shaped similar to an egg, but smaller. Dropping it would be a big problem because she didn't think she could pick it up and make it back to a standing position.

The device looked solid but was actually two pieces. She twisted the top of the egg-shaped device, ninety degrees clockwise, and it lit up. It was yellow for about five seconds and then turned green. As soon as she saw green, she squeezed it with all the remaining strength she had and felt a click from inside it. The neon blue light reappeared and grew to the size of a door.

As her final act, she stumbled through the portal.

The blue light disappeared.

Part One

Chapter One

YEAR 2015

IT WAS A WARM SUMMER EVENING. FIFTEEN-YEAR-OLD DEVIN Baker and his best friend, Sawyer Gomez, were riding their bicycles north on State Street. They'd just left Hill Side Community Church, where they'd been attending a youth group event with over thirty other kids and their leaders. Most weeks, Devin enjoyed the three-mile bike ride. However, he looked forward to next year. That was when he would have his driver's license and would be able to make this trip driving the blue 1979 Ford Mustang that he and his dad had been restoring for the last year.

After the boys left the church, they stopped at the local convenience store on their way home. Every week they came here to purchase a snack for the ride back.

They parked their bikes near the door and out of the way of the fuel pumps. As always, Devin got a bottle of sweet iced tea and a small bag of Doritos, and Sawyer got a packaged ice cream cone.

The cashier, a plump balding man, smiled when he saw them. "I assumed I would be seeing you two tonight. Every Wednesday, the same order."

"No reason to change," said Sawyer.

The boys smiled and headed back to their bikes.

With treats in hand, they continued on their way. Sawyer rode with one hand while eating the ice cream. They passed through the traffic light and down a long winding hill. Next, they would pass the pond where they all skated each winter. Their speed increased as they went down the hill. At the last minute, Sawyer saw a small branch in the road in front of him. There was no time to avoid it, and he probably wouldn't have tried even if he'd seen it sooner. It wasn't big at all. When he hit it, his balance was compromised a little. Not a problem for a teen who was comfortable on his bike, but he'd been paying attention to the ice cream and wasn't expecting it. Startled, he grabbed for the handlebars with his other hand. The ice cream cone broke and struck his thigh before falling to the ground. With minimal effort, Sawyer regained control and didn't even slow down. He was mad, though, that he'd lost his ice cream, which was less than half-finished. Now his hand was sticky from the snack breaking while he was holding it, and there was a big gooey splotch on his pants. Worst of all, Devin had seen it and found the whole thing funny.

"Good job! Is this your first time on a bike?"

"Shut up! There was something in the road."

"That little twig? It looks to me like you just don't know how to ride a bike." Devin laughed.

Sawyer didn't respond right away, but pouted because of embarrassment and the loss of his cone.

After a minute, he said, "Can I have some of the Doritos? I lost my cone and I'm hungry."

"Sure." Devin accelerated to get next to his friend as they approached the curve that went around the pond.

He pulled up next to Sawyer and held out the bag, the same handoff the boys had done many times before. Sawyer took the bag and drifted over a little too close to his friend. Devin responded by veering left, just over the center line as they were going into the curve. At that same time, a car came around the curve, from the opposite direction, and also drifted over the centerline. Devin's bike hit the front corner of the car, throwing him into the windshield, before he tumbled off onto the road. He remained conscious just long enough to feel his left femur break and his head strike the pavement.

The last thing he heard was the woman screaming through her open window and Sawyer calling his name.

Chapter Two

THE FIRST THING DEVIN WAS AWARE OF WAS FEELING COLD, and the next was the bright lights. Slowly the teen regained consciousness. His mouth felt dry and he was disoriented. He saw his mother standing at the side of his bed and Sawyer sitting in a chair, both with concerned expressions.

He closed his eyes, trying to remember what happened, and it all came back to him in an instant. Not only that, but his senses and alertness snapped back to normal.

"Hey, mom." He tried to sit up in bed.

"Lay back. You were hit by a car and you're in a hospital," his mother explained.

"I know, I remember it. But I feel fine."

"Dev, you can't be fine," Sawyer said. "Your head bounced off the pavement. There was blood everywhere. And your leg broke. I saw it. The EMS crew put that splint in your leg while he was still lying in the road." He got up and moved closer to his friend.

"I know. I thought so, too, but my leg feels OK." He looked down at the leg. "Mom, did you call Dad? I don't want him to have to come home early because of this."

"Not yet. He's supposed to fly home from the conference,

tomorrow. When we get the report from the doctor, I'll let him know."

Devin's father worked as a chemical engineer and was attending a conference in Vancouver, Canada. He had left for the event a week before. He was speaking to attendees about industrial solvents, which is something he was frequently asked to do since he was well-respected in his field. This made Devin very proud of his dad.

The ER physician and a nurse walked into the room and slid the privacy curtain out of the way.

"Devin, I'm Doctor Katman. I am glad to see you're awake. I must say, I didn't expect to see you conscious so soon."

The doctor was a middle-aged, medium-height woman with long hair pulled back in a ponytail. She was wearing blue scrubs and a long white lab coat with her name embroidered on the front. She appeared friendly but wore a concerned expression.

"Where are you hurting the worst right now?"

"I don't hurt anywhere. But I remember feeling my left leg break when the car hit me."

"Well, now that you are awake, I'm going to examine you again to find what all is injured."

Once the doctor began examining Devin for the second time, the nurse said, "All his vital signs are still normal."

Nodding, the doctor took hold of his leg and carefully removed the splint. She then pushed and twisted the leg, gently at first, then gradually increased the force.

"None of that hurts?"

"No."

"It certainly doesn't appear to be broken."

Sawyer stepped closer. "I saw the crash and the leg. It broke. I told that to the paramedics."

"The EMS crew mentioned that," said Dr. Katman, "but they didn't find anything either."

"There's no way a leg bends at an angle like it was, and isn't broken."

The doctor looked at him skeptically, then continued her examination. The only reaction she got from Devin was a slight facial change when she pressed on the teen's abdomen.

"Did that hurt?"

"No, not pain. It just feels kinda full. Like pressure."

"Deb, let's get a portable ultrasound in here. I want to get a quick look at his belly."

The nurse turned and left the room to get the equipment.

Speaking to Devin and his mother, the physician said, "So far, everything else looks OK. We're going to get a CT of his head, since he was knocked out. There are a few mysteries here. While you were unconscious, I examined your head. Your shirt is covered in blood and there's matted blood in your hair, but we can't see where it's coming from. Neither of us can find a wound, and there's nothing actively bleeding now. I'd say you and your friend were mistaken about the leg, but I'll get an X-ray just to make sure."

As she was speaking, the nurse pushed the ultrasound machine into the room. She raised Devin's gown and applied green gel to his abdomen before pressing the probe to his skin. After about ten seconds of moving the probe around, she stopped.

Doctor Katman was also watching the screen as she worked.

When the probe stopped moving, the doctor spoke. "There," said Dr. Katman. "Okay, there's quite a bit of blood in your abdomen. I'm surprised it isn't more painful and that your vitals are so good. We're going to get you in for a CAT scan of your head and abdomen and an X-ray of your right leg. While that's going on, I'll page the trauma surgeon so he can come and review your situation."

As the doctor left the room, Lucy stepped closer and took hold of her son's hand. "Are you sure you aren't in any pain?"

"No, mom. Really, I feel fine. What happened to the girl that hit me? Is she OK?"

"Last I saw she was talking to the cops," Sawyer said. "She was kinda hysterical."

"I remember hearing her screaming before I passed out. If the police return during my CAT scan, please have them let her know that I'm fine."

A young woman in maroon scrubs entered the room and got Devin ready to head for the tests. The paramedics had started an IV on the way to the hospital. She now moved the IV bag from the ceiling-mounted hook to a collapsible pole built into the bed, and unhooked the blood pressure cuff and cardiac monitor. She unlocked the wheels and pushed the bed from the room. The medical assistant rolled Devin to an elevator, where they descended one level. From there, it was a brief trip down a bright hall to the imaging area and through a heavy door that read CT 2. The CT or computed tomography is a series of x-rays from multiple angles that allows the inside of the body to be viewed. They brought the surface of the CT table level with the hospital bed and asked him if he could move over on his own. When they were ready, he purposefully used his left leg and pushed to lift his weight and slide over to the hard surface. As expected, he felt no pain from the leg he knew had fractured.

Everyone cleared out of the room so the test could begin. Devin was alone and closed his eyes, thinking about something that had occupied much of his thought over the last month. He remembered back about four weeks ago. He had been at home and needed to slice a lime for a meal he was helping his mother prepare. He cut it in half and then went to cut it a second time, but wasn't paying attention. The blade cut through the lime and right into his palm. He yelped, and dropped the knife, feeling the citrus burn his wound. He hurried to the sink and turned on the cold water and stuck his hand under the stream. To this day, he wasn't sure, but it seemed like the pain stopped just before his palm went into the water.

After a couple seconds, he pulled his hand out to see how bad the wound was, but couldn't find anything wrong. No trace of the injury. But looking back at the counter, he could see the spilled blood. Devin quickly cleaned up the mess. He wasn't sure why, but he didn't want to tell anyone, not even his mother.

His attention returned to the present as they assisted him back to the bed and took him to get an X-ray of his leg. He was confused about what had happened, but there were a couple things he knew for sure—the leg had broken but was now fine. And whatever had bled into his belly was now healed.

Chapter Three

THREE DAYS LATER, DEVIN SAT IN HIS BEDROOM. HIS PARENTS wanted him to take it easy for another day before he returned to school.

The CAT scan showed blood in the abdomen, but no injuries to any internal organs, so they decided to keep him two days for observation, and then sent him home. The doctors who had treated him were all confused by what they were seeing. Devin had enjoyed listening to their theories, and in the end, they told him he'd been extremely fortunate.

Now he just sat on his bed, bored and thinking. He knew something was going on, but he didn't feel comfortable telling anyone. What would they think? Would people become afraid? What if doctors wanted to study him? None of this made any sense.

There was a knock at the door, and Sawyer stepped into the room.

"Hey. Your dad said I should just come up. He thought you were resting."

"Not really resting. Just bored. My parents think I need to rest, but I feel fine."

Sawyer walked to the desk and pulled out the chair. He

removed the stack of folded laundry from the chair and then sat. He caught sight of something bright red in the trash can, which lay between the bed and the desk, and realized that he was looking at several bloody tissues.

"Did you have a bloody nose?"

There was a long pause.

"No, not a bloody nose."

Another pause.

"Can you keep a secret?" Devin asked.

"You know I can." Sawyer looked offended.

Devin stared at his best friend for several seconds, deciding if he should give up his secret. Finally, he grabbed two tissues from the box on the table. He then reached under the blankets and withdrew the razor knife he'd concealed, when he'd heard someone at the door.

"Don't say anything," Devin said. "Just watch." He slid the blade across the meaty part of his palm, creating a one-inch long incision.

"What are you doing!" Sawyer's eyes grew wide.

Devin set the knife down and snatched up the tissues to catch the spilled blood before it fell. He didn't want his mother finding blood on the bed.

"Just be quiet and watch," Devin said firmly. He held the wound out so his friend could see.

In less than five seconds, the incision began closing. In just another five seconds, it disappeared completely. The only trace left was the drying blood on his skin.

"I don't believe it. How did you do that?" Sawyer asked. The amazement was evident in his voice.

"I don't know how or why. I first noticed it when I cut myself a few weeks ago. Before that, I don't know. It seems like I heal quickly from minor injuries. But nothing like this, until recently."

"So this is new?"

Devin thought for a moment. "When I was younger I

needed stitches after a skateboard crash. A couple weeks later, they took the stitches out and the wound was still open a little. So I haven't always been like this."

"This is amazing. Do you feel different?"

"I don't think so. I think I feel normal. Really, I'm just confused. We both know my leg was broken. I felt it and you saw it. By the time I woke up, it was completely fine. I just don't know what to think."

After a moment, Sawyer looked at his friend. "Do it again."

"Do what?

"Your hand. Cut it again. Now that I know what to expect, I want to see it again."

Devin grabbed the tissues and the knife and repeated his demonstration, going deeper and opening a longer incision this time. The outcome was the same. In less than five seconds, there was no trace of the wound.

"Amazing. Did it hurt?

"Sure, for a few seconds. It felt just like any cut you get. But then it stopped and I could feel it closing."

"It's like you're immortal! That's so awesome."

"No, I'm not immortal. Remember how I was knocked out for a while. And you saw how messed up my leg was after the crash. The bones were broken for at least several minutes. If someone shot me in the head or heart, I'd be gone long before I had time to heal. I'm not some superhero. I just heal real fast" Devin explained. He wanted to calm Sawyer's excitement. He may have shared the secret, but he still wanted to keep this strange situation quiet for now.

After a pause, Sawyer said, "Can you do anything else?"

"Like what?"

"I don't know. Like, start fires with your mind, or move objects, or maybe even fly? Can you read minds?"

"I don't know. I hadn't thought about it. I guess I might be able to do other things."

"Let's try," Sawyer said enthusiastically. "Can you tell me what I'm thinking?"

Devin looked his friend in the eyes, and after a minute said, "I'm not getting anything."

"When you look in my eyes, what's the first thing that you think I might be thinking about?"

Devin tried again. and said "Ice cream."

"You did it! That's what I was thinking."

"Sawyer, that's all you ever think about. You always want ice cream."

"OK, try again. I'll think something more random."

Both boys tried for over half an hour, but were never able to reproduce the first lucky guess.

Devin shook his head. "I can't read minds. This isn't working."

"OK, try moving something with your mind. Push that pencil off the edge of the desk."

Devin gave his friend a doubtful look, then focused on the pencil. He closed his eyes and pushed with his mind, but nothing happened. He tried for several minutes before giving up.

"Sorry, buddy, but it looks like healing is all that I do."

Sawyer nodded. "One last thing. Can you un-heal?"

"What is un-heal?"

"Well, if you can heal, can you do the opposite? Can you open a wound on yourself?"

"Why would I want to do that?"

"Just to see if you can."

Devin looked at his friend for a few seconds and then nodded. He focused his attention on the meaty part of his forearm and the skin and underlying muscle split open. Both boys jumped up.

"I don't believe it!" Sawyer said.

They watched as the wound closed up and disappeared.

"You actually did it! This is amazing."

Devin looked at his arm and then at his friend. "I'm not sure what good that is. Batman is very strong. Superman can fly. Me—I can make myself bleed."

"Have you told your parents about this yet?"

"No. I think they'll freak out. I'm sure they wouldn't agree to keep it a secret. They would want me to see a doctor to see if there's something wrong, and I'm not ready for that yet. You can't tell anyone, Sawyer."

He nodded. "So now what?"

"What do you mean?"

"You have this gift… or ability. What are you going to do with it?"

Devin had been trying to find an answer to that question since he'd arrived home from the hospital.

Chapter Four

YEAR 2019

DEVIN'S DARK BLUE MUSTANG CREPT ALONG THE ICY WINTER road. The snow fell thick and heavy, making visibility nearly impossible. It had been storming all night, and now in the early morning it was getting warmer and the roads were slippery.

Sawyer sat in the passenger seat, excited for what the day promised to bring. Both boys were home from college on their Christmas break and were headed to meet some friends they hadn't seen since the end of summer.

Devin and Sawyer had been attending different schools for the last two and a half years, but when they got together their bond was as close as ever. They looked forward to sharing their college adventures when they had the chance to catch up. This time was no different. Last night, the boys had been up until 2:00 a.m. hanging out, eating pizza, and talking about all they had been doing. Sawyer made sure to ask was how things were going with Devin and his girlfriend, Britany. It sounded like their relationship was getting serious.

They'd reluctantly stopped their discussion and gone to bed when they realized how late it had become. The boys had to be up early because they had plans to meet six other high school friends for breakfast. They were now heading to Malcolm Daniele's house. Before changing careers, Malcolm's dad had spent many years as a chef, and he always loved to put on a big feast for his son and his friends.

The boys became aware of movement just ahead to the right. With the snow falling it was hard to tell exactly what they saw, but it looked like a floating human head. Then the white-clad person lunged at the Mustang. Both boys jumped, and Devin fought to keep the car under control and avoid hitting this person.

"Watch out!" Sawyer said.

When they stopped, it became clear that it was a woman wearing a white bathrobe, so she had been invisible except for her head. She was also screaming something at them. Devin's first thought was to get away from this crazy woman. At the same time he was discounting this idea, he became aware that he smelled smoke.

"What are you doing?" Sawyer yelled at the woman, as he got out of the car. "We could have hit you!"

Devin came around the front of the car and saw that the woman was only wearing slippers with her bathrobe. She was so hysterical that they couldn't understand her.

"Slow down," Devin said. "We can't understand what you're saying."

The smell of smoke was stronger now and seemed to be coming from a house tucked back in the trees.

"My house, it's on fire! My daughter is inside! Please help. Megan is inside!"

Sawyer and Devin locked eyes for a brief moment and then sprinted toward the house in the woods.

Pulling his phone from his pocket, Sawyer yelled back at the woman, "Did you call the fire department?"

"Yes, they're coming. But my Megan, she's still in there." The distraught woman answered.

As the boys approached the house, they saw thick white smoke billowing out of the eves on the second floor.

They bolted up the stairs to the wraparound porch. The smoke was thicker here, and as they glanced into the house through the slider, they couldn't see much because of it. What they did see was an orange glow that seemed to be dancing around in the thick smoke. Sawyer grabbed the handle and yanked the glass sliding door, but it didn't move. The woman was catching up. She'd slipped and fallen twice on the way to the house because her slippers had no tread, and the ankle deep snow was quite slick.

"That door is locked!" she shouted.

Sawyer started to head off the porch to find another door, when Devin called to him.

"Stay here." He then looked at the woman. "Where is she?"

"She was upstairs in her room."

Devin backed away from the door about eight feet, then sprinted at it and leaped into the door. The glass exploded. With a painful crash, he fell into an end table he hadn't seen because of all the smoke. He felt the glass tear into his arm and left cheek. He collapsed to the ground as his right ankle rolled. Severe pain racked his body, caused by the impact with the door and the ankle roll, but he had no time to lie there. After leaping to his feet, he moved on and the pain was already gone. He yelled for the girl, but the smoke alarms were blaring and he knew he wouldn't be able to hear if she were answering. Soon, he was hacking and choking. He forced himself to move forward, amazed at how hot it was.

As he approached the steps, he was able to see a little better. There was much more fire here and it provided some illumination. Part of the ceiling had already come down, and he had to move the debris to get through. He could feel the hot items burning his hands. At the stairs, he shoved away a large sheet of fallen drywall and saw a small child underneath.

The collapsed material had opened a large gash on the back of her head and arm. She wasn't moving.

Devin could feel the fire burning his flesh and the searing pain every time he inhaled. He desperately wanted to get out of this inferno. After getting down on the floor, he noticed that the air was much cooler and less smoky. He grabbed the orange blanket out of the girl's hand and covered her with it to provide some protection from the heat. He scooped her up and hurried for the door. Devin moved as fast as he safely could, holding his breath as he forced himself to go through a wall of flames. He didn't know if the girl was breathing. Hopefully an ambulance was on the way.

Sawyer saw his best friend step back onto the deck. Most of his hair and a lot of his clothing had burned away. In his arms was a small body wrapped in a smoldering blanket. Sawyer watched as the hideous burns and blisters on Devin's face disappeared. The two boys lowered the blanket-wrapped form to the ground and unwrapped the girl. Sawyer was trying to remember the differences in how to perform CPR on a child, but it wasn't coming to him now with all the excitement. They were both relieved when they heard sirens getting louder.

The girl looked to be about eight years old, and her head and arm were gushing blood. The boys were relieved to see her chest rising and falling. She wasn't breathing more than eight times per minute, but she was breathing. The boys crouched over her, and her mother was crying hysterically. Devin placed one hand on the girl's forehead and the other under her neck to open her airway so she could breathe better. Her body became stiff for a couple seconds, and the boys watched as the ugly wound on her arm closed up and disappeared. She started breathing more deeply, and in a few more seconds her eyes opened.

Devin let go of her head and stared at the child, amazed at what he'd just witnessed. He pointed to her head and gave

Sawyer a questioning look. From his angle, Sawyer could see the wound better. He looked and moved the girl's hair so he could see the scalp, then looked at Devin with wide eyes and mouthed the word, *Gone.*

When the shock of what he had just seen passed, Devin said, "I think she'll be okay, Mom. Come see."

Still crying, the woman dropped to her knees and took the girl, who sat up in her mother's arms.

Chapter Five

DEVIN AND SAWYER STEPPED OFF THE PORCH AND MOVED AWAY from the house. The firefighters were arriving and the boys didn't want to be in the way. Sawyer started to say something as they were walking away, but Devin gave a firm wave of his hand. He wanted to be sure they were nowhere near anyone who might overhear their conversation. They stepped under a tall cedar tree that was away from all the action unfolding at the house.

"Did you know that would happen?" Sawyer said.

"No! Of course not. That was as much a surprise for me as it was for you."

"Did it just happen, or did you have to tell it somehow to happen?"

"It just happened. I wasn't even thinking about healing. I touched her and it was as automatic as when I heal myself. It just happened."

"Did you feel anything passing between you and her?" Sawyer asked. His questions were coming so fast that Devin barely had time to answer.

Devin paused and thought back. "There was something. I'm not sure what. It was like I felt something leaving me, but I didn't feel weak or drained. I was just shocked at what was happening."

Sawyer shook his head. "That is just amazing. What about you? Looking at your clothes, you should be badly burned. But you're okay, right?"

"It was horribly painful. I could feel my flesh burning, but it was healing almost as fast. I certainly seem to be healing much faster than before." He paused. "Let's try to get out of here. With so much of my clothing burned away, I'm freezing. Let's go back to the Mustang and get back on the road before anyone wants to ask us some questions."

"Sure, let's go."

The boys headed to the driveway and followed it toward the street. They walked past two fire trucks and stepped over a bunch of hoses of different sizes. They were almost to the road when they heard someone approach them from behind.

They stopped and turned, and saw a tall uniformed police officer approaching.

"Boys, please hold up a minute."

"Did we do something wrong officer?" Sawyer said.

"Wrong? Certainly not. It sounds like you're heroes. We just have some questions to ask you."

"Can I go to my car and grab a jacket first?" Devin said. "I'm freezing."

The officer took a closer look at Devin and said. "Are you hurt? You look like you've been burned."

"No, I wasn't hurt."

"I want the medics to look at you before you leave."

"Really, I'm fine. I just want to get my coat on."

"How about while your friend goes and gets your jacket, you and me, we walk over to the ambulance and get you looked at."

"Go on, Dev. I'll get your jacket and meet you there."

Reluctantly, Devin followed the officer. He didn't want to

act as if he had something to hide, but he didn't want all this attention either.

The police officer opened the back doors of the ambulance and Devin stepped in. It felt good to be in the warmth, but it was crowded in there with two paramedics and Megan and her mother. The young girl was lying on the stretcher with everyone else surrounding her.

Her mom grabbed hold of Devin's arm. "Are you okay? You saved her. Thank you!"

He wasn't sure how to respond. "I'm just glad she's doing better." He looked at Megan. "Are you feeling okay?"

"Yes. I keep telling them I feel fine, and they keep looking for something wrong." She sighed.

A short, stocky female medic moved next to Devin. "Where are you hurting?"

"I'm fine, too. No problem"

"Your clothes are mostly burned off. You must have some burns."

Devin pulled off the remains of the long-sleeved t-shirt and stood turning in a circle.

"I was lucky. I didn't get burned."

The medic took a small wet towel and cleaned some of the soot from his skin.

She appeared confused while looking at his arm. "There's blood here." She scrubbed the area with the towel, finding healthy intact skin. To her partner, she said, "It's just like on the girl. Blood but no injury."

The other medic looked up from the laptop he was typing on. "That doesn't make sense. There has to be an injury somewhere."

Sawyer opened the back door and saw how crowded it was, so he said, "I have your jacket and a shirt that was on your backseat. I'll wait out here."

He handed over the clothing and Devin put them on.

"Thanks for checking me over," he said. "Can I go now?"

"Just a minute. I need to get some information for our report, and we want to check your vitals and listen to your lungs."

Five minutes later, Devin stepped out and confirmed with the officer that they could leave. The boys started for the car and were again interrupted by someone coming up behind them. This time it was the little girl's mother.

"Please wait," she said. "I want to thank you both again." She gave each boy a hug. "I don't know what I'd have done if she hadn't made it." She'd started crying again.

Devin put his hand on her shoulder. "I'm just glad we were here and could help."

She took both boys by the arm, pulled them closer, and looked behind her to see if they were alone.

"I know I was hysterical, but I also know what I saw. Your face was horribly burned one moment, and then it was fine. And the spot where the medics found blood on Megan's arm, I saw that it was ripped wide open when you unwrapped her from the blanket. I looked away because it was so gruesome. I couldn't stand to see that injury on my little girl. When I looked back, the arm was fine. I know that sounds crazy. That's why I didn't say anything to the paramedics."

Devin nodded. "I'm glad we were able to help you and your daughter. Will you now do me a favor?"

"Anything."

"Don't ever tell anyone what you saw. People will think you're crazy."

He held up his index finger, and they all watched as the fingertip split wide open and then closed up again. He looked at the shocked woman and moved the same finger to his lips, signaling in the universal signal to keep it a secret.

Devin winked at her, and the two boys walked to the car and drove away.

Chapter Six

ONCE SAWYER SHUT HIS CAR DOOR SHUT, HE BURST OUT laughing. "I can't believe you did that. Did you see the look on her face? Her eyes were open so wide they could've fallen out."

"I know. It was a stupid thing to do. Just felt like a good idea at the moment." Devin joined in the laughter.

"I was almost as shocked as she was. All I keep hearing from you is how it has to stay a secret, and then you do that. You haven't even told Britany, and you think you're in love with her. Was that really the first time you healed someone else?"

"I swear it was. I never even thought it might be possible. I was as surprised as you."

Devin started the engine and the boys continued on their journey. Sawyer pulled out his phone and called Malcolm to let him know they were still on the way, even though they were nearly an hour late, and to make sure some food was saved.

"Have you still not told your parents about this?" Sawyer said.

"No, I haven't. I have no idea how they might take it."

"After what we saw today, I think it's probably time to tell them." Sawyer advised.

"I guess I should. I'll think about it."

The snow had let up, so Devin drove faster. Up ahead was an elementary school whose parking lot was empty because of the Christmas break.

"Devin, pull over in that parking lot for a minute."

"That lot isn't plowed and I don't want to get stuck in the snow. We're late enough already."

"It's not that deep. You'll be fine."

Devin slowed the car. "Why? I'm hungry and we're way late. I'm hoping they saved us some food."

"I want to try something."

Devin didn't say anything else, suspecting where this was heading. When the car stopped, Sawyer unfastened his seat-belt and dug a small folding Barlow knife out of his pants pocket. His father had given it to him as a gift years ago, and he always carried it with him.

He slipped his arm out of his sweatshirt and opened the blade. He put the edge of the blade against the meaty part of his forearm and tried to make a small cut, but found that he couldn't bring himself to slice into his arm. He'd accidentally cut himself with this same knife several times over the years, but to do it intentionally was a different matter.

After watching his friend try several times to cut his skin, only to stop at the last second, Devin said, "Are you going to do this, or can we go eat?"

"This isn't as easy as it looks. How about you do it?" He tried to hand the knife to Devin.

Devin pulled his hands back. "I'm not cutting you. No way! And you better not get blood on my seat."

Sawyer returned his focus to his arm, and after concentrating for several seconds he jabbed the point into his skin and created a tiny puncture. It was so small that it wouldn't even require a Band-Aid.

Devin started laughing. "Really? That's the best you could do?"

Sawyer said nothing and held out the arm. Devin touched his friend's hand. Both boys felt something, and then the small incision was gone.

"What did you feel?" Devin said.

"I felt movement in the wound, the incision closing. At the same time, there was an immediate end to the pain. It all happened so fast."

Devin smiled. "It had to happen fast. That cut was so small it would've healed on its own in another minute or two."

"What did you feel?"

"Same as last time. It was like something left me but was immediately replaced. Even though the injury was much smaller this time, it felt exactly the same. It was a warm sensation, if that makes sense. Not at all unpleasant. If that's all, can we go now?"

"Let's try one more thing first. Try the un-heal."

"You really need to come up with a better term. So you want me to split open your skin?"

"Sure. We know you can do it to yourself. Let's see if you can do it to someone else."

"So, where do you want it? On your throat?" Devin smiled.

Sawyer shook his head. "No, I don't think so. My arm is fine." He held out his arm to his friend.

Devin focused on the idea of splitting open the skin, and touched Sawyer's arm. Instantly a massive wound burst open. It was far more extensive than either boy expected. It was over four inches long and quite deep. Devin lurched back, banging his head on the driver's side window, and Sawyer screamed. Devin recovered quickly and grabbed the arm at the elbow. The horrendous mess of bleeding flesh started closing, and in seconds was gone. Both boys were breathing hard from the shock of what happened.

"Did you mean for that to happen like that?"

Devin looked at his friend and shook his head, still in shock over what he'd done.

"I guess it's a good thing you stayed away from the throat. My head might have been severed." Sawyer joked.

Devin didn't react to the humor. "Can we get going now?"

Chapter Seven

DEVIN DROVE THE MUSTANG DROVE UP THE FRESHLY PLOWED driveway that led to the two-story house that belonged to Malcolm Daniels and his family. There were seven other cars parked in the driveway, and the boys recognized four of them as belonging to the Daniels' family. Devin parked, and they headed to the door. Sawyer knocked, and Scott Daniels, Malcolm's father, opened the door. Before anything could be said, the Daniels' dog, Spike, pushed out to see who was there. Spike was a ten-year-old black and white pit bull who weighed close to a hundred pounds. Anyone who didn't know Spike might be nervous, but once you got to know him, you realized he was one of the most loveable creatures ever made. Both boys had known Spike since he was a puppy and bent down to exchange affection with him.

"Boys, glad you finally made it. We saved food for you."

"Thank you!" they said, in unison.

As they entered the house, Scott said, "Was it the weather? You didn't get stuck, did you? What's that smell?"

They entered the crowded dining room and their five best friends, who they hadn't seen in months, greeted them with loud shouts and waves.

"Glad you finally made it."

"Devin, I thought you could drive in snow. What happened? You're almost an hour late."

"Dev, what happened to your hair?"

The lighthearted comments came from many of the boys, until the smell that Malcolm's father noticed hit the others.

"Dang, guys. You smell like a burning dumpster," Malcolm said. "What happened?"

The group became quiet. The boys realized there was more to this than just simple tardiness, and they wanted to hear the story.

Devin had been thinking about what to tell them, and decided to leave most of the details out to not make a big deal of the situation. He hoped Sawyer would know to go along.

"Back on 34th Street, about a mile south of the elementary school, there was a house fire. We tried to help the lady before the fire department got there. We ended up in a bunch of smoke, and it's all in our clothes and hair."

"Wow, was anyone hurt?" Scott said.

Sawyer answered, destroying Devin's attempt to keep the excitement from the story. "No. And only because Devin here ran into the burning house and rescued a little girl! He lost his hair, and it's a miracle he wasn't burned." He gave Devin a conspiratorial smile.

Devin shook his head. "It wasn't that big a thing. Anyone would've done the same thing."

"Sure sounds like a big thing to me," Tony Jiffers said, and the others all agreed.

"Sounds like you're a hero," said Don Swain.

"Really, guys, it wasn't that big a deal." Devin said as he gave Sawyer a glare that told the other boy to let the story drop.

"Devin, sorry man, but you stink real bad," Malcolm said. "You and I were always about the same size. Let's go upstairs. You shower and I'll dig out some clothes you can borrow."

"Sounds great. There just better still be some food here when I get back."

As they headed upstairs, Devin said, "Where's Tracie today?"

Tracie was Malcolm's sister. She was two years younger than the other boys, but still hung out with them.

"She had her wisdom teeth out yesterday. She's in a bunch of pain and refused to take the pain meds. After being up all night and miserable, Mom made her take the pills a few hours ago. She's finally asleep."

They went into Malcolm's room and he found a t-shirt and a pair of jeans.

"I can give you some socks and underwear, too, if you want. I won't want them back."

"Thanks, but I'll make do with what I have. Can I get a bag to put these old clothes in?"

Devin went to take a shower and Malcolm found him an old plastic bag from the grocery store. Devin stepped into the shower and was impressed at how the smell of the smoke intensified as he started washing. He scrubbed his body several times and then washed the mangled remains of his hair, twice.

While showering, he thought of the implications of the morning's events. He now had an ability that he could do something positive with. He considered going into some kind of ministry to help people. God had given him this gift, and there might be an opportunity to use it to serve.

Devin stepped from the shower and dried with a towel that Malcolm had given him, and re-dressed. He exited the bath-room, carrying the bag with his old clothes. While starting down the hall, he stopped at the closed door to Tracie's room. After pausing for a second, he quietly opened the door. Entered the room and approached the sleeping figure in the bed. The curtains were closed, but there was still enough light to see the bruising and swelling that remained from the removal of the impacted wisdom teeth. He reached down and touched the exposed forearm of his friend. He felt as if something left him, but was immediately replaced. The swelling was shrinking away, and the bruising faded.

Devin turned quickly and left the room. He was concerned that someone would find him in her bedroom and misunderstand his reason for being here. After descending the stairs, he was met by Malcolm's mom, who held up a pair of electric hair clippers.

"Hi, Devin. I hear you had some excitement this morning."

"Yeah, it's been a crazy day, and I haven't even had breakfast."

He heard a door opening upstairs.

"You go eat, and then I'll get that mess on your head a little more presentable."

"Thanks. That sounds good."

Devin continued to the kitchen and heard a cheerful female voice from upstairs call out, "Hey, Mom! Guess what?"

Chapter Eight

GREEN STREET PIZZA WAS A POPULAR LOCATION WITH THE university students. The prices were reasonable, and it was only a short walk from campus. The owner decorated the restaurant with university memorabilia, which created an enjoyable atmosphere.

Christmas Break had just ended, and students were getting back into the routines. They all had new class schedules and had to modify their social lives accordingly. Therefore, this was the first time Britany Murray and her boyfriend, Devin Baker, had enjoyed some time together since before the break. When they arrived for dinner, the restaurant was busy, as always. They found mutual friends at a table and squeezed in two additional chairs to join them. They laughed and joked for a while, but then the others left, leaving the couple alone.

Their conversation had been awkward, with neither of them saying much. They'd caught up on what happened during break and how their families had enjoyed the holidays, but then they were both a bit quiet, distracted with their thoughts. The best part of the conversation had been the watered-down story about the house fire that Devin had shared.

The medium pepperoni and sausage pizza, the couple's favorite, sat between them, half-eaten. They each wanted to bring up something they needed to discuss, but neither felt comfortable doing so in a public setting.

"Is everything okay?" Britany said. "You're very quiet tonight."

"Yeah, I'm just a bit tired. Still getting used to the new schedule."

She nodded. "I am tired, too. I think I'll head back to my apartment and go to bed early."

"Okay. I'll walk back to the dorm and text you later."

Britany stood and Devin gave her a hug and kiss goodbye. He again noticed that she didn't seem herself.

She headed out the door, irritated with herself. She walked to her car and pressed the button to unlock the door. Then climbed in and started the engine.

"Agh!" She yelled as she slapped the steering wheel, even though there was no one to hear her.

She'd intended to tell Devin about an additional detail from the Christmas break, but had chickened out. She had even memorized and practiced what she wanted to say. Now it would occupy her thoughts until she finally did.

All through high school, she had a boyfriend named Trevor. They were inseparable and had even planned to go to the same college. Unfortunately, Trevor was accepted to West Coast University, which they had both applied to, but Britany had been rejected. When it was clear that they would be at schools on opposite sides of the country, they decided to break up.

During holiday break, Trevor stopped by her parent's house. He had decided to transfer to a school that was an easy drive from Britany's school. They were both eager to resume their relationship where they had left off. But there was one detail that Britany had to deal with—Devin. He was sweet and they enjoyed their time together, but what they had was nothing compared to what she and Trevor had shared. She knew that this would surprise Devin and hurt him. She didn't want that, but she was with Trevor again.

She backed out of the parking spot and headed out onto Market Street, her frustration still churning and causing her to be distracted. Not even a quarter-mile from the pizza shop, she failed to stop for the red light at Diamond Street and crossed into the path of a delivery truck. The driver barely got his foot to the brake pedal before his truck impacted with Britany's driver side door at fifty miles per hour. The force of the impact caused her head to strike her side window, shattering the glass violently. The large bumper of the truck crushed the side of the car, forcing the door to intrude into the driver's space by over a foot. This destroyed metal collided with the left side of her thorax, hip and upper leg with devastating results.

Chapter Nine

DEVIN WATCHED HIS GIRLFRIEND LEAVE AND WAS ALSO frustrated. He had planned to have a serious conversation with her, but needed to get her alone. He was concerned about what would happen when he shared his secret with her. However, he knew they were getting closer and closer, and that he could trust her. He had also started thinking about proposing to her at graduation in a little over a year.

On the last day of the Christmas Break, he'd told Sawyer that he was thinking about letting Britany in on the secret. Sawyer had only met Britany once and thought she seemed nice. He'd said that it was up to Devin, but the more people that knew the better the chances were for the story of his healing gift to leak out.

Devin agreed that he wanted to limit the number of people who knew. Currently there were only three, now that he'd told his parents. The night before, he had demonstrated what he could do. They were shocked and had many questions, which he patiently answered as best as he could. Fortunately they saw the wisdom in keeping it secret for now.

Devin still wanted to add one more person in on the secret. As wonderful as he and Britany's relationship was, that wouldn't continue if there were secrets between them. He even decided on how he would tell her. He would give a brief description and then demonstrate it for her, in the same way he'd first demonstrated his ability to Sawyer.

But tonight didn't feel right for that conversation. They needed to be alone for a conversation like this, not in a public place. Devin just wanted to tell her and no longer have this secret between them.

After putting his jacket on and dumping their trays in the trash, Devin headed out the door and watched as she pulled out of the parking lot. While he started walking, he pulled a stocking cap onto his head to protect him from the bitter winter air, there was a horrific crashing sound. It came from the direction Britany had just gone. Moments later, he heard someone scream and sprinted towards the crash. He wondered if the scream had come from Britany. Had she witnessed a collision? As he ran, his mind jumped to another possibility—maybe Britany had been involved in the crash.

It took less than two minutes for him to run the quarter-mile, and as he approached he knew his latter thoughts were correct. A steaming truck and a familiar car sat in the intersection, crushed together. A radio was still on and music could be heard coming from the truck. There were several bystanders, most talking on cell phones, and one taking pictures.

As Devin got closer, he heard a man in the crowd say into a phone, "She was kinda breathing or gurgling when I first got here, but she isn't anymore."

Devin raced to the open passenger door and climbed inside. It was getting dark, but there was enough light coming from the truck's one remaining headlight for him to see that the trauma was extensive. He grabbed her right arm at the wrist and waited, but he didn't feel anything happen. Devin released her arm and then grasped it again. Still, nothing happened. Finally, he took his fingers and felt for a pulse in her neck. There was nothing there.

The horror slammed into his gut. *I was too late. If I could've gotten here faster, I could have saved her.*

Devin had the ability to save many lives, but the one person who mattered the most to him, he couldn't do anything for. He climbed out of the car and sat on the curb, sobbing forcefully.

———

A FEW MONTHS LATER, at the end of his junior year, Devin withdrew from school. He was wasting time. He needed to find out what this gift of his could do.

Chapter Ten

IT WAS A SUNNY SUMMER MORNING WHEN THE DARK BLUE '79 Ford Mustang headed out of the driveway. Devin had been thinking more and more about how he could use his ability and how to maintain control of who knew about it. He wanted to walk into a busy emergency room and start touching injured people, but the security in an ER and the number of potential witnesses made that approach less than practical.

Devin had been excited about the possibility of using his gift as a ministry. But the death of Brittany had him wondering if that was still the direction he wanted to go. The idea of physical and spiritual healing had worked well in his plan, but now he felt derailed by the tragedy and thought a re-evaluation was in order. The one thing Devin was sure of was that until he understood the extent of his abilities, real plans couldn't be made, and he was frustrated because he wasn't sure how to get started.

Last week, Sawyer had helped him design a half-page flyer. It read, *God gave me the ability to heal you. All he wants is for you to know him.* Beneath those words were three scripture verses. He wasn't pleased with it, but assumed that in time he would be able to improve it.

Devin parked in the main visitor's parking lot at North East Regional Hospital. He got out of the car, adjusted his tie, and hurried across the street. Sawyer had suggested that dressing up might make him look a little more official and less likely to be challenged as he moved about the hospital. Devin didn't mind the tie, but he had rejected the suit coat because it felt too stuffy.

Sleep had been elusive last night. He'd laid there thinking about how he was going to approach this hospital visit. It seemed like it was going to be impossible to move forward and still keep control of who knew about his ability. Eventually, he decided to try to maintain his secret a little longer. He fully expected to be escorted from the hospital by security today, but he hoped to interact with at least a half-dozen patients before that happened.

Devin walked through the entrance and past the security guard. He continued on without looking at the guard, his heart rate increasing. Because the lobby was torn up for remodeling, he had to walk across sheets of plywood. There were giant sheets of plastic blocking off parts of the large room, and the smell of paint was prominent. Devin kept his eyes forward and marched on. He figured that if he looked like he knew where he was headed, less attention would be drawn to him. The elevator was ahead on the left. By the time the car finally arrived, no one had even given him a second glance. He pressed the button for the third floor, and before the doors closed, two other people got in. The first was a man in his mid-fifties, wearing a faded t-shirt and ripped blue jeans. The second was a short woman in her late twenties or early thirties. She had Hispanic features and was wearing green scrubs and a lab coat with a stethoscope hanging out of a pocket. She had a backpack over her shoulder, and her left arm was in a sling.

The man pressed the elevator button marked 5. The woman just glanced at the buttons and did nothing, clearly satisfied with one of the two floors already selected. The elevator stopped on the third floor, which was for patients who were recovering from surgery. There were several different units here, so there would be a wide variety of health issues Devin could encounter.

He exited the elevator, followed by the woman, and paused to look at an electronic directory mounted on the wall, showing the different units on this floor. A3 was off to the left and it seemed to be a good place to start. He headed in that direction, now following the woman with the sling. Devin slowed his pace so she wouldn't be too close as he tried to determine which patient to visit first. He passed through the large open doors and could see that there were about twenty or more patient rooms, with a nurse's station in the center. Looking into the first room he came to, he saw there were a bunch of people inside. Several hospital staff members and a few visitors all in conversation. That was precisely the type of room he wanted to avoid.

Devin looked into the next room and was disappointed to see it was empty. There were only a few more options close by, and then there were some patient rooms directly across from the nurse's station. Again, a place he wanted to avoid. For the third time this morning, he considered turning around and going home. He was getting more and more nervous.

A patient occupied the third room and there were no visitors. He entered, trying to look like he belonged. A middle-aged African American man was resting, reclined in the bed. There was an IV pole next to the head of the bed, with several fluid-filled bags of different sizes hanging from it. A tray table containing a cup of ice, a cell phone, and a magazine sat next to the bed, all within easy reach for the patient. The patient was awake but seemed sedated. He didn't focus on Devin as he walked in.

"Good morning," Devin said. "I'm stopping in to see how you're doing and to leave you something to read."

"Thanks. I'll look at it when I'm a little more awake."

"Do you mind if I ask what brought you in here?"

"My appendix. I waited too long to come in and it ruptured. I guess if I'd come in earlier it would have just been a couple small incisions. Instead, since it ruptured they had to slice me wide open."

Devin moved closer to the bed. "OK. You get some rest."

He touched the man's arm and felt a familiar sensation. Something left him and was instantly replaced.

"What happened?" the man asked. "I suddenly feel much better."

Devin could tell that he was still lethargic from the lingering effects of the anesthesia and pain medication.

"Get some rest, and if you're still curious later, read the paper I left. I only ask that you please don't tell anyone I was here, for a while."

He turned and walked out, smiling at the confusion on the man's face.

Devin decided it would be best to get away from the site of his first healing. He moved to the next hall, which was marked B3. This area had a similar configuration. It was an elongated U-shape, with the nurse's station in the middle. As he was approaching the first room, a nurse and a male visitor came out. She was giving him directions to the cafeteria as they walked past Devin, who quickly stepped into the room. In the bed was a woman in her mid-thirties. Her left leg and arm were immobilized and packed in ice packs. She was sitting up and working a TV remote in her right hand.

"Hi, I'm just coming around to drop some paperwork off," Devin said.

"Okay, just set it down and I'll look at it later."

"May I ask what happened?"

"I was on my motorcycle and a car backed out of a drive-way, right into me."

"Oh, no. It looks like you got it pretty bad." Devin moved got closer to the bed.

"Yes, I did. My stupid leg broke in three places, and the arm in two. They did one surgery on the leg and another on the arm. There are going to be at least two more on each once the swelling goes down. I'll end up with lots of pins, plates, and screws."

"Maybe that won't all be necessary." Devin took a final step closer and gripped the woman's uninjured arm.

"What are you…" All her pain was terminated, and she felt movement inside her injured extremities.

Devin released his hold on the woman and smiled. "How does it feel?"

"What did you do to me?"

"Take a look at your bad arm. How does it seem to be doing?"

She reached over and took the ice packs off, and uncov-ered it as much as she could. Some of the bruising was still there, but it was much better, and the swelling had decreased considerably. Most noticeable was that the arm was straight, no longer bent and broken.

"Try moving it a little," Devin said.

The woman gave Devin a questioning look, then slowly made a fist and then opened it and then closed it again more quickly. She started moving the wrist, feeling no pain. She took her eyes off of the healed arm and looked at the young man that had just shown up in her room.

"Is the leg fixed, too?"

"Yes. There won't be any more pins and screws."

"How did you do that?"

"God gave me a gift—the ability to help others. Please read the sheet I brought. Also, the hospital will probably throw me out of here when they notice what I'm doing. Please don't say anything for a little while. I want to help a few more people."

As Devin left the room, he heard a sincere, "Thank you," called out to him.

He started toward the other side of the unit to look for his next target, unaware that he'd already attracted attention.

Chapter Eleven

DR. ROBYN KELLER WAS IN A TERRIBLE MOOD. THE throbbing pain in her left wrist seemed to be getting worse. Maybe it had been a mistake to try to start back to work today. She'd stopped taking her pain medication last night, knowing that she couldn't return if she were still on it.

Two days ago, she'd been jogging on the trail around the lake after leaving the hospital in the evening. The weather had been perfect and her mind was still on work. She jogged this trail often and knew every twist and turn completely. As always, she had her earbuds in and was listening to her favorite jogging playlist. She was coming upon a sharp bend in the trail and was adding power to her run as the incline increased. Suddenly her right foot slid out from under her throwing her balance off. She fell and hit the ground with her left arm out in front of her. The pain exploded into her wrist. She rolled onto her back, screaming.

After composing herself, she slowly sat up, wondering what had caused her fall. That's when the smell hit. She looked back down the trail and at the disgusting mess on the bottom of her running shoe. Robyn felt rage when she realized she was the victim of an irresponsible dog owner who'd failed to clean up after their pet.

She struggled to her feet and started the mile-long walk back to her car, the swelling in her wrist increasing constantly. Tears streamed down her cheeks, and she thought about what damage there might be and how long it might take for her to recover fully. As a surgical resident, the use of both hands was mandatory. An injury like this could significantly damage her career.

That evening, the X-rays showed that nothing had broken. It was a bad sprain and should heal without surgery. She was prescribed pain medication and told to keep it iced for twenty-four hours, which she'd done. However, she needed to return to work, even if she wouldn't be able to get any operating room time. She'd be stuck following up on patients that other surgeons had worked on, and that irritated her more than a little.

So as she was pulling into the staff parking lot, into a spot reserved for physicians, she was again thankful that it was her left wrist. If it had been the right, driving would have been much harder. After she parked, she reached into the back of the car, got her backpack and slung it over her shoulder. She swiped her badge and entered the building through a staff entrance. After passing down a long hall, she walked through the doorway to the locker room designated for female physicians, and went to locker 39. She opened the door and placed her small purse inside, which contained her wallet and car keys. She took out her white lab coat and checked to make sure her stethoscope was in the front left pocket of the lab coat where it belonged. She then thought better of it and moved it to the right where it would be more accessible. She carefully removed the sling and slowly worked the injured arm, with its immobilizer, through the armhole.

As she was fighting with the lab coat, the locker room door

opened and Danyle "Danny" Klock entered. She was another surgical resident. Robyn and Danny were friends who occasionally got together outside the hospital.

"What on earth did you do?" Danny asked as she opened her locker, four down from Robyn's. "I heard yesterday that you were off the surgical rotation for a while. They wouldn't tell us why."

"I fell while running and got a nasty sprain. Don't think I'll need surgery."

She didn't need to be known as the surgeon who sprained her wrist from falling over dog poop, so she left out those details.

"That sucks. I hope it doesn't cause you too much trouble with your rotations. I've already had several of your cases assigned to me."

"Yeah, that's my concern. I'm not sure how long I will be out of the OR, or what this'll do to my schedule."

"If I remember correctly, I warned you about the hazards of jogging."

"Yeah, I knew you were going to mention that." Robyn finished getting her lab coat on and the sling reattached.

"Let me know if you need anything. I need to get up to two. I have a cholecystectomy scheduled in forty-five minutes. I'll text you later." Danny grabbed her bag and headed out the door.

Robyn shut her locker, awkwardly shouldered her pack, and left a couple of minutes later. She entered the main lobby and went to the bank of elevators that would take her to the post-surgical units. As she approached, the elevator opened and she followed two men into the waiting car. One was in a t-shirt and ripped jeans. The other was young and well-dressed. He was even wearing a tie. At first she thought he was probably clergy, but then noticed that he wasn't wearing the purple lanyard which designated that role.

She glanced at the elevator buttons and saw that her floor was already lit up. When the doors opened, the better dressed of the two men exited ahead of her and paused to look at the screen that displayed a map of the floor. As she was about to offer him directions, it seemed he'd figured out where to go and he started walking. She continued on her way, now ahead of him. She was aware that he was following her, clearly headed to see someone on A3. She moved behind the desk at the nurse's station and sat her backpack on an available chair.

"Doctor Robyn, what did you do?" asked Sherry Taft, the administrative assistant assigned to this unit.

She was a large, pleasant African-American woman. She was always friendly and not at all intimidated by the difference she had from the physicians on the corporate ladder.

Sherry's words were loud enough that several nurses and another physician heard, and they all came over to find out what was happening. Robyn paused for them to gather, and then told all her co-workers the same modified story she'd given to Danny in the locker room. They were all sympathetic and supportive, and Robyn was glad to have the news out. The sooner everyone knew, the sooner she could stop explaining it. After some additional small talk, she grabbed the chart for Wayne DeVaul. He was one of her surgical cases and should be going home soon. Mr. DeVaul had come in with a cancerous tumor on his right kidney, and Robyn had been on the surgical team involved in removing it.

After taking the chart, she crossed the hall and walked up two rooms to where her patient was. That's when she noticed the guy from the elevator. He was leaving a patient's room. Maybe he was clergy, after all.

Wayne DeVaul was sitting up in bed, with his wife in the chair next to him.

"Wayne, how are you feeling today?" Robyn said.

"Much better. They're telling me that I should be able to go home this evening."

"That's the plan. I'm just going to check a few things to make sure everything still looks good."

She had her patient roll up on his side, and pressed on his abdomen and side just above the hip. She was pleased that it wasn't painful. She then examined the surgical incision and saw that it seemed to be healing well with no sign of infection. The examination was a simple process that she'd been doing for years, but now was quite awkward using just one hand. She lowered the patient's gown and stepped back.

"You can roll back now. The incision is healing nicely. The lab drew some blood earlier this morning. If that also looks good, I don't see any reason why you won't be able to go home later today."

"That's great," said his wife. "He hasn't been getting much sleep here. I'm sure he'll rest better at home."

Robyn nodded. "That's often the case. Which is one of the reasons why we want to get people discharged as soon as medically appropriate, and today looks like your day."

As she turned to leave the room, Wayne said, "I hope your arm isn't hurt too bad."

Robyn realized that she would be telling the story over and over again. "It's just a simple sprain. I'll be able to use it again in a week or two."

"Oh, good. I'm glad it's nothing worse than that," the wife said.

After leaving the patient room, Robyn returned to the nurse's station, where she sat at the desk, made a few notes in the patient's chart, and clumsily entered instructions in the computer with one hand. In less than ten minutes she was done. She checked the computer and saw that her next patient was in room B3. She slung her bag over her shoulder and walked down the hall toward her next patient.

Approaching the nurse's station for this unit, she saw the same well-dressed young man walking out of another patient's room. He headed down the hall, deeper into the unit. Robyn went to the nurse's station and deposited her bag. She was about to reach for her patient's chart when she recalled something she'd learned at a recent in-service. *If someone is behaving strange enough that you notice, it should be reported.*

This guy wasn't behaving strangely... or maybe he was. She didn't think it needed to be reported, but she felt that she needed to investigate this herself. It would probably be nothing, but what if it was something nefarious and she didn't say or do anything. Ignoring the chart, Robyn followed the path he'd taken down the hall. She peeked into three rooms and he wasn't there.

She started to enter the fourth when she heard a voice say, "Please don't tell anyone I was here. I want to stop and see more patients before they throw me out."

When Robyn heard this, all the pieces fell into place. This guy was here either preaching to strangers or trying to hustle them! She entered the room and saw the young man in the tie holding up a pamphlet and encouraging the patient to read it.

"What are you doing here? You can't be bothering patients in their own rooms. You need to come with me. You need to have a conversation with hospital security!" Robyn could feel the throbbing in her wrist increasing.

"Doctor, you don't understand," said the woman lying in the bed. "Look here."

Robyn looked at where the patient was pointing. Her left leg was exposed. Robyn was about to ask why she was looking at the leg, when she noticed there were large bloody pads next to her upper thigh.

"What am I looking at?"

"I was hit by a car. I had compartment syndrome. They had to slice open the whole upper leg so I didn't lose circulation. They were waiting for the swelling to go down to close it up and repair the knee."

The patient lifted the leg and rotated it several times. It looked healthy and responded normally.

"When was this?" Robyn asked.

"Last night."

"That isn't possible."

"I know. But he touched me and it closed up, and the pain is gone. I also had a burn scar here on my arm. It was from when I was a kid. It's gone, too."

She exposed her arm. There was nothing there.

Robyn moved around to the other side of the bed to better look at the leg and the bloody pads underneath it. The intruder followed her, but Robyn halted and spun toward him.

She held up her hand in a clear sign to stop moving, she commanded, "You stay there. You're not to touch any patients."

He finished the last step he was taking and grabbed her outstretched hand. She tried to pull it away, but his grip was tight. He held on for only a second or two and then released her.

The young man smiled at her. "Dr. Keller, I'll be out in the hall when you're ready to talk." He turned and left the room.

Robyn was confused. Something had happened, but she wasn't sure what. And then it hit her—the constant throbbing was gone. She looked at her wrist and then at the patient.

The look of confusion on her face must have been evident. The patient looked at her and smiled, and said. "Your arm stopped hurting, didn't it? I know it's impossible, but he did it to me, too."

Robyn carefully moved her wrist, a little at a time. She unhooked the sling and removed the immobilizer. The swelling was gone. She started flexing her hand a little more, and then twisted it to the left and then to the right. The pain didn't return. She walked over to the tray table, picked up the pamphlet, and skimmed it before setting it back down.

"Are you OK?" she asked the patient, a quiver in her voice.

"Never better."

"OK, I'll have someone come in and check on you."
Robyn exited the room.

The patient, indeed, never had been better. She worked
for a TV news station, and many of her colleagues had
already visited her and could testify to her injuries. This story
would be huge, and she'd be right in the middle of it.

Chapter Twelve

DEVIN STOOD IN THE HALL, WAITING FOR THE WOMAN WHOSE lab coat read Dr. R. Keller, to come out of the patient's room. His hands were sweating. He had known this would all come out eventually, and it seemed that now was the time. He thought about how he needed to be bold and confident, but he wasn't sure he could pull that off.

After almost a full minute, she exited the room, carrying her sling and wrist immobilizer. The confidence she had when she'd first walked into the room was gone. She was visibly confused and seemed apprehensive.

"What's your name?" Doctor Keller asked.

"Devin Baker."

"Devin, what did you do in there?"

Devin smiled. "You can feel and see it for yourself. I healed you."

"How many patients have you touched?"

"Four. Plus you."

"How did you do this?"

"I really don't know. All I do is touch people, and they're healed. Now that's all I have to say. I want to discuss this with whoever is in charge."

Robyn nodded, thinking about the request. She wasn't taking a kid to hospital leadership with the wild claim that he could heal with a touch, even if her wrist seemed fine now. Also, considering what she'd witnessed, she couldn't have security escort him out of the facility.

"Before I take you anywhere, I need to see this for myself. I'm not going to come off as a nut with some outrageous story about something that I haven't even seen."

Devin nodded. "I understand. It's all quite strange. Even I'm still getting comfortable with this whole thing. Follow me."

As they walked up the hall, Robyn felt irritated that this guy had somehow taken control of the conversation.

Devin led her into an empty patient room.

"There's no one in this room," she said.

"I know. Let me see your hand."

"Why?"

"If you want proof, show me your hand."

She did as he'd asked. Devin took her wrist with his right hand and rotated it so that the palm faced upward. He took his left index finger and touched her palm. At the same time, he tightened his right-hand grip just enough so she couldn't move her arm. An incision about an inch-and-a-half long opened up on her palm, and she tried to pull away.

"Just watch," Devin commanded.

She stopped resisting and stared with wide eyes as the opening in the flesh began to disappear. Devin released his grip. Robyn jerked her hand back with a look of shock, and examined the spot where moments ago the skin had been split open.

"Convinced?"

She nodded. "How did you do that?"

"Honestly, I have no idea. I wish I knew."

After a short pause, Robyn walked out of the room. "Follow me."

They headed back toward the elevators and heard some

commotion back near the nurse's station. They couldn't understand everything they were hearing, but it was about a specific patient and they did catch the words *miraculously healed*. Upon hearing this, Devin smiled. Robyn didn't.

As the elevator moved, Devin thought about this unplanned situation. He only intended to try to heal a couple people and leave, but now he had to improvise. An opportunity had developed, and he decided to try to make something of it. He had known that this would have to happen at some point, but his plan had been for things to move a bit slower.

"Devin, why are you here? Are you just trying to heal a few people, or is there more to this?"

"This whole healing thing is new to me. I'm trying to understand it."

As the doors opened, Dr. Keller looked at Devin. "I'm not screwing up my status in this hospital. You keep quiet and let me talk first."'

"No problem. I don't want to cause you any trouble."

She looked at the man who had healed her wrist and thought that it was already too late for that. There would be many conversations about what he had done here today, and she had stumbled into the middle of it. Then she considered her wrist and how much inconvenience Devin had saved her, and felt her frustration with the situation decrease.

They entered the large office area of Hospital Director, Dr. Stephen Collins. His administrative assistant wasn't at her desk, so Robyn walked into the director's office.

She looked at Devin, and said, "Wait here." Then shut the door in his face.

Devin was initially shocked, but then began to understand. She was stuck in an awkward position and needed to protect herself. Introducing him to the man who probably was her boss's, boss's boss could be a significant risk for her professionally if it turned out that Devin wasn't as special as she thought. He would make sure not to say anything that would cause her embarrassment.

After just a couple minutes, the door opened and Robyn waved him in. "Devin, this is Doctor Collins. You wanted to talk to someone in charge, and this is him."

Devin walked up to the director and held out his right hand. "Glad to meet you, sir. I'm Devin Baker."

Dr. Collins took the offered hand and immediately felt a sensation he couldn't identify. Feeling something also, Devin widened his eyes, wondering what he'd just healed. Neither of the men was aware that the peptic ulcer that caused frequent discomfort in the doctor's stomach would never again be a problem.

"Devin, Doctor Keller here is saying some outrageous things about you. She had me call down to 3B and they're also saying somethings that don't make much sense."

"I understand that, sir. Please know that Doctor Keller just happened to fall into this. Her first concern was that no patients were harmed, and then she had a tough decision as to what to do with me."

"Thank you, Devin," said the director. "She says you can convince me as to the legitimacy of your claims."

Devin rotated his own right forearm so the anterior surface faced upward. He then took his left index finger and traced a line halfway from his elbow to his wrist. As he did, the skin and muscle spilt open.

"What are—?"

"Just watch," Robyn Keller said, responding before Devin.

As the wound started closing, Dr. Collins moved forward, studying the process. Devin could see the doctor's mouth drop open in amazement as he observed.

Wide-eyed, he stared at Devin. "That's incredible! How do you do that?"

Devin smiled at the simple question, "Honestly, I have no idea."

"And you can do that to other people, too? Not just yourself?"

"Yes, I demonstrated that to Doctor Keller."

Director Collins looked at the surgical resident, and she nodded. "He did the same thing, but on my hand."

"Is this something you've always been able to do?"

"Doctor Collins, how about we sit down and I tell you the whole story?"

The director dismissed Robyn to return to her duties, asking that she not discuss what had happened. Then Devin and Dr. Collins sat, and for fifteen minutes Devin gave an in-depth explanation of what he'd been experiencing. As they spoke, the director pulled up the hospital records from Devin's admission five years before and read about the incident that occurred at the beginning of his fantastic story.

"Devin, that's fascinating. I guess my first question is, why are you here? What is it that you were trying to get out of your visit today?"

"The honest answer is, I'm experimenting. I believe that this is a gift from God, but I still don't fully understand what it is I can do. Can I fix brain or spinal injuries? What about disfigurements from years ago? What happens if I touch someone who had a leg amputated? I doubt it will grow back, but what will happen? I recently saw a dog that was hit by a car and had a leg injury. I stopped and touched him, but nothing happened. I need to understand these abilities, and I'm hoping you'll help. I need to know what I can do so I can make a long-term plan as to what to do with this ability."

Devin took a deep breath. He felt like he was talking too fast, and he hoped this hospital director would be willing to help.

Chapter Thirteen

KEVIN MCDONALD DROVE THE FAMILIES BLUE 2019 FORD Edge out of the airport parking lot. He was exhausted and would be glad to get home. He glanced over at his wife, Carla, and knew she felt the same way. It had been a long day. The American Airlines flight was supposed to get in four hours ago, but there had been a mechanical problem and now it was after midnight. Their four-year-old son, Cooper, had been great through all this and fell asleep within a few minutes of being strapped into his booster seat.

Cooper wouldn't be happy in the morning. They'd been telling him that when he woke up in the morning, Domino, the one-hundred-ten pound black and brown German Shepherd, would be home with him. Cooper and Domino were inseparable, and the absence of his best friend had been tough on the toddler this last week. Since it was now so late, picking up Domino from the kennel as planned wasn't possible.

Carla had initially been concerned about having such a big dog around a young child, but from the day they brought Cooper home from the hospital, Domino had adopted him as his own and was amazingly gentle with the boy.

This family vacation wasn't something they'd planned.

Kevin worked as a detective with the county sheriff's department and was assigned to the narcotics division. He'd been the lead detective in a two-year investigation that ended up arresting over twenty gang members and confiscating close to $30 million in heroin and fentanyl. The arrests all happened about nine months ago. Just over a week ago, the trial of the gang leader concluded and the jury decided that he would spend the rest of his life in prison.

Following the sentencing, there were several threats of violence made against Detective Kevin McDonald, who had faced the cameras following the arrests. Some of the threats were from gang members with dangerous pasts, and Kevin's superiors recommended that he take a paid vacation for a week and let the anger against him subside.

They had decided to fly to Dallas and visit Carla's family. It had been almost two years since they'd visited, and she missed them and wanted to show them how much Cooper had grown. The trip had gone well, and the vacation had been restful and fun for the whole family. During Kevin's absence, the sheriff's department hadn't heard of any more threats and things seemed to have gotten back to normal.

"How are you doing? Too tired?" Carla said to her husband, after they'd been driving for twenty minutes.

"Not bad. It will just be good to get home and sleep in our own bed tonight."

"True. But it was good to go visit. I was missing them all, especially my parents. I know they enjoyed seeing Cooper."

"It was a good week, and Coop did great with the traveling, time changes, and disruption to his routine. I was really proud of him."

Carla asked her husband, "Do you think things have settled down here?"

"I sure hope so. I just want things to get back to normal."

They continued in silence for a couple minutes and stopped at a red light. As they waited, Kevin became aware of sound and motion to his left side. He glanced over and saw a motorcycle pulling up next to him. The bike had a sleek low-profile design and was built for speed. There were two people on the bike, both covered in leather. A tall thin man drove and a medium-height woman sat on the back, their faces partially obscured by bandanas.

As soon as the bike came to a stop, they both drew handguns. Kevin spun in his seat and grabbed Carla by the front of her jacket, and while fighting both of their seatbelts, did his best to force her to the floor and lay over her. The gunshots were extremely loud, but he could still hear and feel all the glass shattering, and a round grazed his exposed right shoulder.

The attack only lasted a few seconds, and then he heard the bike's engine roar as it pulled away. Kevin sprang up, released the seatbelt and put the Edge in park. Ignoring the pain in his shoulder, he pulled his off-duty weapon from the concealed holster mounted under the dashboard and rolled out the door. He fired four rounds at the fleeing bike. The first of the .40 caliber rounds hit the frame. The second and third entered the back of the rider and passed through her and into the driver. The forth only hit the driver because the woman had fallen off. Kevin rose from his crouched position, watching as the motorcycle keeled over and tumbled down the road. Neither of the riders moved from where they'd landed.

After turning back to the car, Kevin saw Carla still slumped over, held up by her seatbelt. Two bright red growing stains were visible on the left side of her chest. She was alive and struggling to breathe. Kevin looked into the backseat at Cooper, who was screaming. His head and arms were covered with small cuts from flying glass, but other than that he seemed to be uninjured.

Kevin threw himself behind the wheel, ignoring the shards of safety glass digging into him and the pain in his shoulder.

He closed the door, threw the car in gear, and stomped the accelerator.

"Hang on!" he said to his wife as the car rapidly accelerated, unsure if she could hear him. "The hospital is just two miles from here."

A minute and a half later, they pulled up at the Emergency entrance. Kevin leaped from the car and sprinted into the building, screaming for help.

Chapter Fourteen

DEVIN SAT AND TRIED TO RELAX, BUT THAT WAS IMPOSSIBLE. Glancing over at the speedometer, he saw that it read a little over 100 mph. He tried to think about what he was about to do, but the constant sound of the siren wouldn't let him concentrate. Part of his problem was that only four minutes earlier, he'd been sound asleep.

The last two weeks had been a whirlwind of activity for him. North East Region Hospital was one of twenty-seven hospitals owned by a parent company. Because of this, they were able to share resources and personnel. This brought costs down and allowed for more specialized care to be available in smaller hospitals. The interaction between the hospitals also brought Devin and his amazing ability to the attention of many people. Since first meeting Director Collins two weeks ago, he had visited over a dozen hospitals and rehabilitation facilities. During that time, he'd had four helicopter flights and two round trip flights on private jets. He thought he could get used to this excitement.

Unfortunately, while his meals and lodging were all paid for, they weren't paying him for his time.

He'd made clear the things he wanted to try, and they also

had other ideas of their own. The results had amazed everyone. He'd touched close to a hundred people. He saw paralyzed people walk, and trauma patients on the brink of death sit up and talk. One man who'd been in a coma for five years, opened his eyes and spoke.

Devin had also attended many meetings where they discussed his abilities and how to best utilize them. All those conversations always came back to the impact Devin's talents would have on hospital revenue. At first, Devin was amazed that this would be such a significant concern. Then one of the hospital administrators sat with him and explained how much financial damage his ability could have.

"They told me this is about another officer's wife. Is that true?"

Devin's attention snapped back to the present. He glanced over the stern-looking police officer, who drove. She appeared to be close to his own age, early twenties.

He thought about her question and tried to remember. He had been asleep when he heard his cell phone ringing. He fumbled for it in the dark and answered it, noticing that it was a little after 1:00 a.m. The person on the other end had introduced themselves, but Devin didn't remember the name. He thought they said that they were a doctor with Yankee Medical Center. They said something about a woman involved in a shooting, and they didn't believe that she would survive surgery. They told him that he should get dressed fast and that his ride would take him to a Life Flight helicopter. He fumbled to get dressed, still processing what was going on. As he ran down the stairs, he could hear sirens approaching. He yelled to his parents that he had to leave for an emergency. He ran out of the house as the police cruiser came to a stop on the street. Its red and blue lights were reflecting off the neighbor's homes in the dark. He jumped into the front passenger seat and it raced away from the curb before his door fully shut.

"I was sound asleep when they called me," Devin said. "All I remember is that a woman was shot."

"What are you? Some kind of special doctor?"

"Something like that," Devin said, not wanting to have to explain more.

The cruiser came around a curve in the road, and ahead was the local park. The lights of the landing helicopter illuminated the parking lot.

As soon as the car came to a stop, Devin called, "Thanks for the ride," as he leaped out the door and sprinted toward the aircraft.

He made sure to approach from the front of the helicopter, staying away from the deadly tail rotor that even he wouldn't survive contact with.

A hand reached out the side door. Devin grabbed it and someone pulled him inside. The door slid shut and a helmeted figure directed him to a seat, where he assisted Devin in getting strapped in. Once the buckle snapped closed, the aircraft lifted straight up. The seat was small and uncomfortable, having folded down from the wall of the helicopter. Soon, he felt them banking and the forward motion increasing. The lighting in the cramped compartment was minimal, and someone handed Devin a headset, which he fumbled with for a minute before getting it on correctly.

"Devin, can you hear me?" a male voice said, through the headset.

"Yes, I can hear you."

"OK. My name is Tommy. I'm one of the flight medics. My partner is Duane. We have about a fifteen to twenty-minute flight."

"Is there any way to get an update on the injured person?"

"I will see if I can get some information," the medic said.

Tommy adjusted something on the radio console, and then he was talking again, but Devin couldn't hear what was said.

After a couple minutes, Devin's headset came on again,

and he heard Tommy say, "Devin, I've got Yankee Medical Center on the line. They can hear you."

"Hello?" Devin said tentatively.

"Devin, this is Doctor Philameni. We spoke on the phone."

"Yes, Doctor, I remember. I was asleep when you called, and I'm not sure if I caught everything. Can you give me an update?"

"Certainly. The patient is a twenty-nine-year-old female with two gunshot wounds to the left lateral chest. She's extremely unstable. She'll die without immediate care, and the trauma surgeon thinks there's probably too much damage for her to survive the surgery. The surgeon met you last week and he's the one that insisted we try to get you here. He was afraid that if he opened her up, there would be so much blood loss that their team wouldn't be able to deal with all the damage in time. Since you're on the way, he's trying to delay opening her, but he's prepared if she crashes. This really is an every-second-matters situation."

"I understand. I'll be there as soon as possible. Please make sure there's someone there to lead me to her."

"They're already on the roof, waiting."

Devin handed the radio handset back to Tommy and sat back. He thought about Britany and how he was just seconds too late. He felt a cold terror, knowing that it might happen again.

Minutes later, he felt the wheels touch the roof and he shot out of his seat and yanked the lever that held the door closed. He jumped down and sprinted across the roof toward the door and the elevator beyond, where someone dressed in hospital scrubs waited for him. The elevator felt like it was hardly moving as it slowly descended.

When the doors finally opened, Devin and his guide sprinted down the hall. They took a right turn and saw another similarly dressed person waiting by the entrance to the operating room. She held a blue surgical mask in her hand.

"Put this on and then go through that door."

Devin complied, though not sure of the purpose of the mask. They'd already learned that he could cure infections.

He pushed through the door and entered the scrub room, where all the sterile gowns, caps, and shoe covers were lined up on shelves inside boxes. He continued past several large sinks and pushed open the doors to the OR and continued toward the feet of the woman on the operating table. He listened to what the surgical team was saying, and was shocked at the sounds of panic as they frantically tried to save their patient. These skilled professionals were clearly fighting a losing battle and they knew it.

"She's losing too much blood!"

"Her pulse is only in the forties and dropping!"

"This isn't working."

"Who is in charge here?" Devin said.

Everyone looked at him, and one spoke from behind his surgical mask. "Devin, I'm Doctor Mills. We met last week."

Devin recognized the voice, and a face came to his mind. They'd sat and talked for a while last week and then ran some tests together. He had liked Dr. Mills and had enjoyed working with him.

"When I do this, everything will close up," Devin said. "You need to get everything out of her first."

While frantically working in the woman's chest, the surgeon replied, "We can't. She'd bleed out before we got it all unhooked. Can you do your thing in small increments"?

"I will try, but I've never done that before," Devin explained.

Devin used his index finger and tapped the woman's leg. He then waited a few seconds and repeated the action. With each tap, Devin felt a familiar sensation.

"Is anything happening?" he asked.

"The bleeding is stopping. I see things moving in here!" said the surgeon. "Things are healing. Keep doing it the way you are."

Slowly Devin tapped, and gradually all the sponges, clamps, and other things Devin couldn't identify were removed from the open chest cavity.

After a couple minutes, Dr. Mills said, "OK, Devin. We're all out. Finish her up."

Devin stopped tapping and gripped the woman's leg, and in ten seconds it was all over.

Dr. Mills removed his surgical mask, smiled, and nodded his thanks to Devin. The rest of the staff in the OR stared in amazement at what they'd just witnessed.

Devin took a deep breath. He felt relieved, but also a little bitter. For this stranger, he had made it just in time. But for Britany, he had failed.

Chapter Fifteen

EARLY ONE MORNING, A COUPLE WEEKS LATER, DEVIN LAY awake in his bed, thinking of all he'd learned. He had recently completed all the experimenting with the hospital group, so he had a clear idea of what he could and couldn't do to heal people. The results of the testing indicated that the life of the injured tissue was the most critical factor. If the muscle, nerves, or bones were still alive, then he could make amazing things happen. If the cells within the tissues had already died, there was nothing he could do.

He had tested on a patient who experienced brain death following a drowning. Nothing had happened with his touch. Another patient who had suffered some lesser brain damage following a high fall got back almost all functionality.

Now it looked like his work with the hospital group might be at an end. At first there had been lots of excitement about his healing of Carla McDonald. Some physicians were making plans for how to utilize him on a regular basis. Then the board, which oversaw the twenty-seven hospitals, started questioning the legal ramifications and financial impact of using Devin's abilities. And the next thing he knew, all the previously open doors had been shut.

This was of minimal concern to Devin. He'd gotten most of what he wanted, and he had never envisioned working in a formal hospital setting. He now has an understanding of precisely what he was able to do. Even with a clear understanding of his capabilities, he still wrestled with how best to use this gift. The problem remained that there was no way to move forward and not have his ability become public knowledge. The last thing he wanted was for strangers to be camped out on his lawn, begging to be touched. He couldn't do that to his parents.

As he contemplated this, he heard Chief, the family's young black Lab, start barking. Then Devin heard someone opening the front door.

Seconds later, he heard, "Devin! Please come down. There's someone here for you."

Reluctantly, Devin got up and dressed before descending the stairs. As he neared the main floor, his father, Randall Baker, looked up at him.

"It looks like it happened a little earlier than we expected. There's a news crew out there."

"Really? I had thought we'd have a little more time."

"I know," his father said. "What do you want me to do?"

"I'll deal with this. You don't need to get caught on a camera."

His father nodded, and as he retreated to the other room, Devin opened the solid wood door a crack so he could see out. The first person he saw was a woman who looked familiar, but he couldn't place where he had seen her. She was dressed in a skirt, blouse, and heels. Next to her stood a man in a shirt and tie. He held a microphone, and Devin knew he had seen him on the news before. Standing behind him was a more casually dressed woman holding a video camera.

Devin cracked the door a little wider, making himself visible to the three. As soon as he did, the man with the microphone stepped forward.

"Mr. Baker? I'm Al Bixton with TV16. We've heard about what you're able to do and we'd like to interview you. This is an amazing story, and our viewers would like to know more."

Devin could tell from the red light on the front of the camera that they were recording him.

"Mr. Bixton, I have no idea what you're talking about. Please leave."

Devin started to close the door, when the reporter said, "Mr. Baker, do you deny giving this pamphlet to my colleague here, when you miraculously healed her last month?"

Devin stopped and looked back at the reporter and the woman beside him. She held one of the flyers he'd handed out in the hospital. Then he recalled why he knew her. She was the woman with the leg injury. A car had hit her and her leg was severely damaged. In fact, she was the woman he was helping when the surgical resident Dr. Keller had caught him.

Unexpectedly, Devin found himself improvising again. He pointed at the woman he'd healed. "You, inside the house! You other two are not coming in."

"Mr. Baker, we would just like to speak to you for a minute so we can report on this amazing story," said Al Bixton.

"She comes in now and alone, or I shut the door and speak to none of you."

"Can she bring a recorder?" said the woman holding the camera.

"Absolutely not!"

The trio of intruders started whispering among themselves.

"The door closes and locks in four seconds. 4… 3… 2…"

"Okay. Just me, no recording."

The woman stepped forward, and Devin held the door open for her.

As she stepped inside, he looked at her comrades. "You two don't have permission to be on the property, and you certainly may not try to look in my windows with that camera." He slammed the door and locked it. In a menacing voice, he said, "Give me your phone now."

"My phone? Why?"

"Now!"

"Okay, okay. Here it is." She handed it to him, and he set it on the end table by the door.

He wasn't going to take any chances that she might try to record the conversation.

"Follow me." Devin led her to the dining room, because the living room had large windows, which someone could easily record video through. He closed the drapes, making sure they had their privacy. "Have a seat."

She sat in a straight-back wooden chair.

"What is your name?" Devin said.

"Candice Adams," she replied, with a tremor in her voice.

She could see that Devin was furious, and she had no experience dealing with situations like this.

Devin raised his left hand, his palm towards her face. His palm split wide open, causing Candice to gasp in shock. Once his hand returned to normal, Devin took his index finger and placed the tip firmly on her forehead. Candice's eyes grew wide in fear, not knowing what he might be able to do.

"Tell me now, do you have any recording devices on you?"

"N-no, sir. I don't. I promise."

Devin removed his finger. "Good." He walked around the table and sat across from her. "So Candice, it appears that it was a mistake on my part to help you."

"No, it wasn't. I am very thankful. If it weren't for you, I would still be in the hospital and I'd be having more surgeries scheduled."

"So you're thankful, and to show that, you invade the privacy of my home? If you air a story about me, there will be dozens of other reporters here at my parent's home, and hundreds of people showing up at all hours, wanting me to touch them. Did you think of that?"

"I hadn't really thought about that. This isn't something I do. When I told them what you did, they were excited about the story." Candice tipped her head toward the front yard.

Devin looked at her, confused. "I thought you were a reporter."

Candice shook her head. "No. I work for TV16, but in the IT department. I'm a database administrator. After my accident, a bunch of my coworkers came and saw me in the hospital. They knew I was badly injured. The next day I showed up at work, fully restored, and with an amazing story. There was no way to keep it quiet."

Devin thought about what she'd said and wasn't sure how much this changed things, if at all.

In a voice lacking all the venom he had earlier, said, "You see, Candice, as soon as a story about me gets out, I have to move out of my parent's house and find someplace to stay that's either secret or has lots of security to keep everyone away. I'm not going to live with a constant stream of people following after me, wanting me to heal them."

"OK. But sooner or later, this will come out. The only way to keep it secret is to never use your ability again."

Devin nodded. "I know. But I need time to get some things in place. Things like a new residence, and figure out how I'll get around privately."

"That makes sense. But at some point, you will end up going public. Correct?"

"Sure. I don't think there's much else for me to do, as far as learning my limits. The next step is to start using it."

"What if you were to partner with TV16?"

"What do you mean?"

"We agree to back off and leave you alone until you're ready. You agree to talk to no other media until you're ready to work with us. Then together, we host an event where you heal a bunch of people and we record the event and interview you. That way, you'll know who you're dealing with and you'll have more control over how your talents get revealed."

"Will your station agree to this?"

Candice smiled. "I'm friends with the production manager. I know how they think. I'm sure they will love it. For us, we get the exclusive story without having to sneak around and have you hate us. I really can't speak for the station, but I'm sure they'll go for it."

Chapter Sixteen

SIX WEEKS LATER

DEVIN GOT OUT OF THE CAR CARRYING A SMALL BACKPACK. TV16 had provided a vehicle, a driver, and a plain-clothed security officer.

"I'll be back in a few hours," he said to the men.

"Yes, Mister Baker," the driver said. "We'll be here to get you back to the apartment."

The partnership he'd worked out with TV16 had proven to be more valuable than he'd expected. Not only had they found him temporary housing that included security. They were also helping him find a more permanent residence. He needed a place to live that was gated, with security. Most homes like that had long waiting lists.

Devin was having an exciting morning. He had just come from the TV station, where he'd recorded an interview for broadcast later that evening. He had reviewed and approved all the questions ahead of time. His biggest concern was that they would go off-script and try to probe in areas he wasn't yet ready to disclose. Fortunately, they kept their word and stayed with the planned questions. Now he was walking into a nice hotel, on a beautiful late-summer day, where they would have, what they were calling, their Unveiling Event.

Devin entered the spacious lobby and saw Candice Adams waiting for him. The station had pulled her from her usual duties and assigned her as an official station representative for Devin. During the last weeks, they had become good friends. While there was nothing romantic between them, they worked well together and Devin had come to trust her.

"Hey, Devin. We have everything set up. People are starting to arrive."

"Sounds good. Where do we go?"

"Follow me. I have a small room for us to wait in while everyone is still arriving."

She led Devin to a small conference room adjacent to the large meeting room. Devin peeked into the larger room and saw many people seated, including his parents, who were sitting in the back. They insisted on witnessing the event. The TV station had agreed, and Candice had joked that they would only charge them half-price.

"How many people did you guys invite?" Devin said. "We agreed on a hundred fifty. Looks like there are far more than that in there now."

"Well, the word got out and we had a few more inquiries after we did the screenings. There are actually a hundred sixty-four. Also, we told each of them that they could bring someone with them if they wanted."

Devin nodded. "A hundred sixty-four, and they are all paying two hundred dollars?"

"Yes, that's the deal, and you get half. The station gets the other half, but we cover all expenses." She confirmed.

Devin nodded. He would walk out of here with over $16,000. Furnishing the secure house that the station was helping him find would be no problem if he could do this a few times.

Candice had set up a team whose job it had been to find 150 good candidates to see Devin at the Unveiling. Devin had provided specific criteria about the conditions he could heal.

He was nervous enough tonight and didn't want anything to come up that he might not be able to successfully cure.

Devin took a seat and accepted the offered water bottle, but passed on the snack foods.

"Devin, do you mind if I ask a question?" Candice said.

"Of course not."

"Every time I see you, you have long-sleeve shirts on. It has been over eighty degrees out for the last week, and still the long sleeves. Is that because of your ability?"

"Yes, when I was working with the different hospital teams, I had a couple incidents where someone brushed up against me. Once in a crowded room, and twice in an elevator. All three times, I felt the sensation that I had done something to them. Two of them reacted, clearly aware that something happened. I don't know what I healed. Maybe just an old scar, but I decided that I wanted to control who I was contacting. So I started wearing long sleeves. I also try to avoid shaking hands or any other casual contact."

After about fifteen minutes, Candice received a text message which said that everyone was seated and ready to begin.

"OK. You're up," Candice said.

Devin opened the backpack and took out a large packet of the flyers he'd been handing out at the hospital. Someone from the station would be giving them to each person as they left the room.

Candice and Devin exited and made their way to the meeting room, where Devin walked to the front. There were temporary lights set up, and TV Cameras there to catch the healings from all angles. Someone from the station handed him a small microphone that he clipped to his collar. He received a nod from a member of the sound team.

"Hello, My name is Devin. I want to apologize if I seem a little nervous. This is the first time I've done this publicly. I have been given a gift from God—the ability to heal. I know it sounds crazy, but in just a minute you'll see how real it is. When you leave the room, someone will hand you a pamphlet. I ask that you take one and spend some time reading it in the coming days." Devin looked at Candice and nodded.

She also had a microphone. "Will everyone in group one please stand and line up here."

As soon as the first ten people got in line, someone led them to the front and Candice took the sheet of paper that they each held.

She glanced at the papers. "Devin, this first man is Jim. He is a retired firefighter. He inhaled fire while on a call. His lungs are severely damaged, and he also has some facial burns."

The man, who appeared to be in his early fifties, hesitantly walked up and smiled nervously. Devin could see the burn scars on the face of the man, who was also on oxygen because of the lung damage. He carried a small oxygen tank in his left hand.

"Jim, please face the audience," Devin said. As soon as he turned, Devin touched his exposed arm.

The audience members in the front rows, who were close enough to see the burn scars disappear, gasped. With wide eyes, Jim removed the oxygen tubing from his nose and took two slow, deep breaths. Then the tears started flowing, and he embraced Devin.

"Thank you. Thank you so much!"

As Jim released him, Devin heard Candice say, "Next is Kate. She was struck by a car years ago, and was severely injured. She is in this wheelchair because of the severe back pain she has when she walks. This is from the many vertebrae that were broken in the accident."

Devin looked at the pretty girl, who appeared to be in her mid-twenties, and seemed frightened.

"Are you ready to be out of that chair?"

She nodded tentatively.

Devin held out his hand and she took it. He didn't help her up immediately, but waited for a familiar sensation to pass. By then, he could already see the delight on Kate's face and helped her to her feet. She slowly twisted, then turned and bent forward and touched her calves, and then sprang up and gave Devin the second of many hugs he would receive that day.

Part Two

Chapter Seventeen

YEAR 2106

THE MORNING STARTED LIKE ANY OTHER FOR DR. MATTHEW Becker. He awoke, showered, and got ready for work. Hugged his two adolescent children goodbye and watched them head outside to catch the bus to school. His son, Ralph, was fourteen years old, and his daughter, Deb, was sixteen. Within a few minutes, he watched the fully automated bus pull up out front. On a signal from the navigational computer, the door opened to allow the students on. As Matthew watched the bus drive away, he thought back to his youth, when there had been so much debate about allowing robobuses to transport students. It took several years for the technology to mature, but now it was as common as all the other automated cars on the road.

The bus scanned the implanted biochip in each student's right arm as they each entered and exited the vehicle. Cameras monitored the student's behavior, and penalties for infractions were severe. From a single control center, a handful of people monitored entire fleets of buses. In some more problematic districts, an adult attendant rode. Not to drive, but to deal with discipline problems.

As he watched the bus leave, Matthew's wife, Mallory,

walked up and stood next to him. She worked in administration at the local hospital, and she worked from home most days.

"Do you think you'll be late tonight?" she said.

"I can't think why I would. I've got some exciting stuff going on, but nothing that would keep us there late. I'll be in the lab all day, except for my lunch with Brian."

"Are you retrying the experiment today?"

"We plan to try a couple of variations on what we did on Friday.

"Is there any reason to expect different results?"

"I doubt it. We just need more data so we can figure out what's going wrong."

"Okay. Good luck. I'll see you when you get home."

They kissed goodbye, and Matthew stepped outside just as the car pulled up at the curb. His eyes widened when he saw that this morning he had a yellow car. Yellow was an uncommon color for cars. Most robocars were generic gray. He could remember only a few times he'd ridden in a one this color.

He got into the backseat, glanced at the status panel in the front, and saw that all the lights were green. A few days before, the car that picked him up had two amber fault lights showing. One had a low fuel indicator, and another for a secondary communication failure. The cars were supposed to fuel themselves, if needed, before any assignment and take themselves out of the rotation for any errors on their systems.

Twenty years ago, private automobile ownership started being discontinued. Massive pools of autonomous vehicles replaced privately owned one. These autonomous vehicles were on the road constantly, moving from one job to the next. No longer did private cars sit idle in driveways for hours to days at a time.

He sat back and relaxed for the fifteen-minute ride as the car's virtual attendant updated him on recent sports, news, and weather. Matthew rested his head back and closed his eyes, absorbing the information the attendant was feeding him. Occasionally he would say, *"Skip,"* if the article being presented was of no interest.

The attendant was interactive, and Matthew could make inquiries to the system. The virtual attendant would locate any requested information and display it on built-in screens or deliver it verbally. When the car scanned his biochip as he entered, it accessed his online profile and knew the information he would most likely want to hear.

During the trip, Matthews's attention was caught by a fleet of large pilotless drones taking off from a retail distribution center. Once they'd gained altitude, they all split up and headed in different directions toward their assignments. They were either headed to stores to deliver their product, or to a delivery company that would get the merchandise directly to customers.

As they were nearing the lab, Matthew said, "Stop presenting."

The attendant stopped talking.

"Attendant, reserve a car for 11:45 to pick me up at work and take me to the Lobster House restaurant in Jamestown."

"Reservation made and added to your schedule," said the vehicle attendant.

"Message Brian Stoffer and inform him that I'll plan to meet him at about noon." Referencing the information in Matt's biochip, the virtual attendant found the entry for Brian Stoffer in his online address directory."

"Message sent," The automated voice said.

Matthew and Brian first met at a conference five years ago and had become fast friends. Since they worked close to each other, they arranged to meet for lunch three to four times each year. Matthew always looked forward to these opportunities to see his friend and catch up on what they each were doing.

The car arrived in front of the unimpressive office building.

Matthew got out, and a voice from inside the car said, "Have a good day, Doctor Becker."

He entered the building and passed the reception area. Approached the transparent panel that blocked access to a specific area of the building. Querying the biochip in Matt's right arm, a computer that controlled building access instructed the panels to split apart and let him pass. Matthew continued down the hall and took an elevator down two levels. He exited and went to his office, where he deposited his jacket.

"Attendant, are there any messages for me?"

"One message from Brian Stoffer," said a voice coming from a small device on his desk. "It says, 'Sounds good. See you then.'"

Matthew went to a panel on the wall. It slid open, and he took out a mug of hot coffee. When the systems recognized him enter the building, it waited one minute and then had the hidden coffeemaker in the panel prepare the coffee so it would be ready when he arrived. He left the office and entered the lab, carrying his mug.

"Hi, boss," said a chorus of voices, as he entered.

"Morning, guys. Are we ready?"

"Let's do this," an enthusiastic team member replied.

"OK, just like last time. You send at 8:15, and we will receive at 8:10."

Three of the team members left with two boxes, headed to the other lab on that floor. The first of the boxes contained a toy metal truck, a plastic horse, and a watermelon. The other contained an instrument package that included a small power source and dozens of sensors that measured environmental conditions. The teams were about to repeat an experiment they'd tried the previous week, where they'd successfully moved the three objects back in time. It had only been a five-minute time jump, but it had proven that they could do it. Unfortunately, there had been complications. This time they would also send the instrument package back. Hopefully it would help them understand what the objects experience when going back in time.

Everyone's attention focused on the workbench in the center of the room. Two of the remaining team members setup video recording equipment surrounding the workspace. At precisely 8:10, a neon blue pinpoint of light appeared a couple inches above the workbench. It rapidly grew to a foot high and two-feet long. Within the light, several items appeared, and then the portal disappeared. No one approached the bench. They were waiting for the scanning to complete. The team scanned the new arrivals for over a dozen factors, including temperature, radiation, static electric charges, weight, and molecular density. Once the computer signaled the all-clear, they could all see that just as last time, things weren't perfect.

The transition across the timeline worked and the truck and the plastic horse looked as expected. But the watermelon was now a sloppy pile of goo that continued to decompose as they watched. These results were the same as last time. The instrument package seemed fine, and a team member took it so the data it had collected could be analyzed. Hopefully, it would shed some clues as to what had caused such a negative impact on biological matter.

"I guess it isn't ready for human trials," a voice said sarcastically.

Doctor Matthew Becker considered responding to the comment, but refrained.

"Remember, people," he said, "this is what we expected. Not what we hoped for, but we knew this was likely, based on last week. Let's go through the same analysis as before. Maybe we'll find something we missed last time. Once we have the results from the instruments, we will let you know what we found. We'll run the next test after lunch. Let's plan for that to start at 1:30 p.m."

With the apparent problem in sending biomatter across time, the team wanted to conduct another test. They would transmit six new objects this afternoon—a fresh cut stick from an oak tree, a piece of wood from a 2X4 that was several years old, and well dried out., a potted plant, a raw chicken leg, an apple, and a cup filled with water. Some members of the team wanted to place a goldfish in the water, but it was decided that they would get a better understanding of what worked and what didn't before adding a living organism.

Chapter Eighteen

AT 11:45, MATTHEW BECKER WALKED OUTSIDE HIS OFFICE building and saw a car pulling up to the curb. It was basic gray and appeared to be one of the newer models that he'd begun seeing late last year. As he approached the car, the vehicle scanned his biochip and then opened the door for him.

He sat, and the virtual attendant said, "Good morning, Doctor Becker. Has your destination changed, sir?"

"No change."

"Very good. We will arrive in approximately fifteen minutes."

Looking out the window, Matthew appreciated the beautiful sunny fall day. This was his favorite time of year. He far preferred the cooling temperatures to the hot summers here in Eastern Virginia.

Returning his focus to business, Matthew took his pocket comp and began reviewing the test data. The pocket comp is an advanced pocket-sized computer and communication device. It interacts with the implanted biochip that everyone gets injected in their arm at a young age.

The test this morning had the exact outcome they had

expected because they'd run the same test the week before. The problem was that the examination of the watermelon following the first test showed the destruction of most of the plant cells. At the cellular level, there was something about the time travel process that was incredibly destructive. Since the eventual goal was to be able to move a person through time safely, this was a big problem they needed to solve.

The instrument package they transmitted today recorded everything possible, and the results had become available just as Matthew had to leave for his lunch appointment. The second test later that day would involve a wide range of organic materials, and they would study the effect of time travel on each.

As Matthew studied the test results, he noticed that almost everything seemed to remain normal, with the exception of atmospheric pressure and friction. Both had spiked off the chart for the fraction of a second that it took to move from one time period to the next. Maybe this information and the next experiment would give them a path to eventual success.

The vehicle began slowing and Matthew shut off the pocket comp.

"We're arriving at your destination, sir."

"Has Brian Stoffer's car arrived yet?"

"Yes, sir, it has. The restaurant reports that he has been seated."

The car stopped along the street and the door opened.

As Matthew got out, he heard, "Have a good day, Doctor Becker."

He walked down the short footpath that led to several restaurants on the waterfront and entered the Lobster House.

He approached the console inside the door and before he could say anything, an electronic voice said, "Welcome to the Lobster House, Doctor Becker. Doctor Stoffer is already here. Please follow the blue light."

Matthew didn't think much about the efficiency of the system. He'd grown up with this technology and would have been surprised if it didn't all work correctly. As soon as the car had arrived, it transmitted his biochip's identification code, his name, and on-file payment options to the virtual attendant at the restaurant. The virtual attendant identified him as soon as he walked through the door. The payment information received from the car meant that other than how to split the bill, there would be no need to discuss payment.

A blue light appeared on the floor and Matthew walked toward it. As he approached the light, it moved along the floor, remaining about eight feet in front of him, leading him to his seat. It continued until it reached a table with an ocean view. As Matthew approached it, the light disappeared.

The restaurant was decorated with a classic nautical theme. There were old buoys, flags, and parts from old ships, including porthole windows, propellers, and steering wheels hanging on the walls, along with digital images of old boats scrolling on several screens around the restaurant.

Seated at the table was his good friend Brian Stoffer. Brian was a tall, thin man in his mid-fifties, with dark skin and a southern accent. He was the president and CEO of Stoffer Medical Enterprise (SME), which was involved in all areas of health care. Brian personally oversaw the medical research division and had secured multiple federal grants for various projects he had underway. SME had a reputation for acquiring the best talent and coming up with impressive results.

Brian stood as his friend approached, and the men embraced warmly.

"Matthew, I'm glad you're here. It's been too long since we last met up."

"I know, I know. Things get so busy, and the next thing I know we haven't met in months."

The men took their seats. They had a great view of the pier and some boats in the distance.

The two of them spent the next few minutes discussing family and recent vacations while looking through the electronic menus on screens built into the tabletops. Eventually, Matthew motioned toward the small box in the center of the table, while looking at his friend. Brian nodded, indicating that he was ready to order, and pressed the button on the box.

"Attendant take orders," Brian said. "separate bills."

"Doctor Stoffer, go ahead and order."

"I will have the seafood jambalaya with iced tea."

"Seafood jambalaya with iced tea. Your order is submitted. Doctor Becker, please place your order."

"I will have the sea bass with rice and mixed vegetables, and I'll have iced tea, too."

"Understood. Sea Bass with rice and mixed vegetables. Your order is placed. Your beverages will be out shortly. Do either of you wish to add an appetizer?" the mechanical voice asked.

Matthew looked at his friend, who shook his head.

"No," Matthew said.

Two minutes later, a waiter appeared with their drinks. As soon as he left, Brian got to the meat of the conversation—the progress in their areas of research. The two loved to know how each other was progressing and what they'd accomplished.

"So Matthew, how's your time travel work progressing? The last we talked, you hoped to be able to open a window into the past, soon."

"We did that. At first, it was quite small and we could only open it for a fraction of a second, but our team succeeded in sending a focused laser beam through the small opening. We were able to send it back an hour. Later, we tried to send it back a day and found that it doesn't matter how far back we send it. It's just as easy to send it a month as an hour. Since then, we've been working on creating a larger, more stable portal. Last week my research team successfully transported three objects in the lab back in time fifteen minutes." Matthew explained.

"That's amazing! Are you getting close to being able to send a person back in time?" Brian asked.

"Well, that's where we're stuck. Objects made of metal or plastic move back easily, even electronics. However, biomatter is a problem. Something happens during the move between time periods that's extremely destructive to organic material. We sent a watermelon back, and when it arrived it looked as if it had spent time in a food processor. Most of the cells had collapsed, and we watched under a microscope as the remaining ones disintegrated over the next hour."

"Ooh, that's a problem. What've you done to try to figure this out?"

"Not much. That first watermelon test was only last Friday. We repeated the test and got the same results again this morning. This afternoon we'll try again with a wide range of other organic materials to see if the results shed light on what's causing the problem. We expected hurdles, and this is just one more for us to clear. We'll figure it out." Matthew explained.

"One of my teams is working on new ways to treat radiation poisoning. As I'm sure you know, radiation exposure destroys the cells in the body. They're working on a treatment that will strengthen the cells and prevent their destruction when exposed to radiation. If you want, I can set up a meeting between that team and yours to see if there might be a place where their work might help with yours," Brian offered.

Matthew nodded. "That would be great. If you can explain to them what we're trying to do and have them call me, that might be very helpful."

"Glad to help. You've come so far. I'd be glad to do anything to help move this along."

"What about your work? How is it progressing?" Matthew asked.

"Much slower than yours, I'm afraid. Like I told you before, we're looking for a formula that will allow the human body to heal at a must faster rate than is currently possible. Unfortunately, that's not easy. We haven't had any real progress lately, just a few theories based on our studies."

"What kind of theories?"

"Well, in order for the body as a whole to repair at a faster rate, the changes we make have to impact the entire body at the cellular level. We have an early version of a serum, that when applied directly to a group of cells, increases their ability to repair themselves at a fantastic rate. The problem is that it's extremely slow to penetrate the cells to make the changes that are needed."

"OK, I'm following you. How slow are you talking about"?

"We desire to have a drug that can be injected into someone who's seriously injured and have their rate of healing increased by ten or even a hundred times. We have a formula that we think will work, but because of how long it takes to spread through the cells, the actual healing of the entire body wouldn't even start for years, or maybe even decades."

"Oh, I see where that's a problem. But it seems like you have a start on your journey. Just need to work some of the problems out," Matthew said, trying to be encouraging.

"Maybe. But even if we get this problem resolved, we still don't know for certain if the formula will work to allow injuries to heal faster. We can't test that part until we get past this first roadblock," Brian explained with the frustration evident in his tone.

"It looks to me like we're both chasing some exciting

things at the cellular level," Matthew said. "I say whichever one of us finishes first, doesn't have to pay for lunch next time."

"I suspect that I'll be the one paying, but I accept." Brian said.

Chapter Nineteen

SANDRA SAT IN THE FRONT SEAT OF THE VAN. NEXT TO HER was Darrel Benning. She despised it when she had to work with him. He was cruel and always made crude comments. The worst part was his apparent aversion to bathing. His hair was always greasy, and she doubted a comb had ever passed through it.

The van had the markings for a home maintenance company that didn't exist. They had applied the labels to the sides of the vehicle when they were halfway there and would remove them in a few hours.

They mentally prepared themselves, since they were nearing their destination. The van had driven them the seventy-five miles to the subdivision. It would return them in just a few hours. The trip back would be longer. They would head about thirty minutes in the opposite direction before finding a secluded spot to remove the decals from the vehicle. Then they would head back home. Once they had returned, they wouldn't just erase the navigational computer. They would replace it with a new one, and the current one would be shredded. No record of their early morning mission would exist.

Sandra instructed the vehicle to kill the headlights just before the van pulled up to the house. She looked over at Darrel, who nodded, indicating that he was ready. He was dressed identically to her. They wore one-piece, skin-tight containment suits. Between the suits, gloves, and shoe covers, no evidence would be inadvertently left behind. They each had a wide band around their forearm to shield their biochips. It would be disastrous if systems in the house scanned them.

After exiting the vehicle, they each strapped on a power belt. Sandra carried a small bag made of the same material as their suits. Nothing would come off the bag that could be recovered by law enforcement. As they approached the house, they each put on a tight-fitting hood which connected to the power belt. The hood was airtight, and the power belt would run the small built-in air re-circulators built into their face-masks. When they left here, there wouldn't even be any exhaled air left behind that a crime scene unit might be able to detect, capture, and analyze.

As they silently approached the single-story house, they moved as quietly as possible and watched the neighboring houses to make sure they weren't attracting any attention. Darrel took a device and placed it against the lock, and a few seconds later they heard a dull thump as a circular hole with a three-inch diameter was blasted through the steel door, shattering the lock. Sandra pushed in first, with her electric baton held in front of her. She didn't mind what they were about to do—it was a necessary task. But Darrel's eagerness disgusted her.

She quickly figured out the layout of the house and went to the bedroom of the immaculate home. The target was starting to get out of bed to investigate the sound from the door being blasted open when Sandra entered. Sandra had the baton's voltage set to three, and delivered a shock intended to daze but not cause much pain. The woman collapsed back onto the bed, and Sandra knelt next to her. She grabbed the woman's pocket comp, which was on the stand next to the bed, and helped her sit back up.

"We don't want to hurt you. So you will follow our instructions, or this will become a very painful morning."

The shocked woman just nodded.

"All I need you to do is call in sick to work. Can you do that?"

"Yes." The trembling woman nodded.

Sandra handed her the pocket comp, and the woman took it and made the call, during which, Sandra could hear Darrel digging through the drawers in the kitchen. She knew his twisted ways and had no intention of letting him torture the woman.

As soon as the woman hung up, Sandra placed the baton on the woman's chest and pressed the button again. It was now on its maximum setting of twenty-five. She died instantaneously and rather painlessly.

As Sandra put away the baton, Darrel entered the bedroom, carrying a large meat cleaver.

"What? Is she dead already? I was planning to have fun with her!" Darrel said, the disappointment evident in his voice.

"Relax. You'll still get some sick fun."

Sandra was glad the woman lived alone. Otherwise this would have been a lot messier.

She took a small case from her bag and removed the laser scalpel from the inside. Rotated the dead woman's right arm so the anterior surface faced upward, and then felt the flesh for a few seconds, before finding what she wanted. The laser scalpel lit up with an almost undetectable hum, and she adjusted the laser beam to be about a quarter of an inch long. She made an incision in the arm, about two inches long. She returned the laser scalpel to its case and put it back in her bag. Then she took a small specimen cup and squeezed and prodded at the incision until she removed a tiny device about the size of a grain of rice. The biochip had been in the woman's arm for over thirty years. It was an early version, one of the first million chips produced. Sandra placed it in the specimen cup, sealed the cup and put it into her bag, then stood and looked at Darrel.

"Do your thing. They need at least a day before it becomes clear why this happened, so try to keep my incision from being noticed right away. Remember, no evidence gets left behind or taken out with you."

"I know. I have done this more than a couple of times before."

As Sandra left the room she said, "The problem is you enjoy it too much."

She looked over her suit. It was clear of contamination. All she found was a little blood on her gloves. She went to the kitchen and washed her gloves to get them as clean as new, while trying to ignore the chopping sounds coming from the other room.

Chapter Twenty

PEGGY WILSON APPROACHED HER DESTINATION—BURLESON Park in Gila Bend, Arizona. She rode a twenty-five-year-old Honda motorcycle built in the year 2081. Coincidently, that was the same year that Peggy had been born. While non-autonomous vehicles were still legal, they were less and less common. She knew that anyone seeing her bike would notice that it was under manual control, and that could stand out. While being noticed on this trip was undesirable, it was far less of a concern than the idea of a log from an autonomous car being able to track this trip.

Peggy was a slightly shorter than the average woman, with long brown hair and a bubbly personality. She was independent and always tried to get the most out of life. This trip was the fourth one she'd made to meet her contact. If she saw anyone other than the man she knew as Bobby, she'd get back on the road and get out of there quick.

Bobby would recognize Peggy's motorcycle. She'd taken it to all of their meetings, which had been in a different location each time. He'd even commented on the excellent condition that such an old bike was in.

As always, Peggy was a little concerned with what Bobby

would ask her to do. Each time they met, he wanted something else. And each time, he gave her a considerable amount of money for her trouble. None of this made any sense to her. She hadn't told him anything overly secretive. For the most part, the information was benign, and much of it was available from one of many publicly accessible online sites.

Today she felt more concerned because Bobby had been adamant that the meeting take place today, late in the afternoon. She couldn't shake the feeling that this was something different.

Most of the money she'd received from Bobby sat safely in an anonymous offshore account that he'd assisted her in setting up. She hoped to use the money for an early retirement.

Peggy had started her job a little over two years ago. She worked as a lab technician for a company called Argon Technologies. They claimed they were working on developing immunizations for livestock, under contract from the Department of Agriculture. But she didn't believe that. Internally, there was water cooler talk that the Department of Defense was paying their bills. This made more sense to Peggy because the lab was hidden and had armed guards. Also, she worked in a facility containing a Level Four Bio-Hazard environment. She had trouble understanding the need for those kinds of precautions for experimental animal vaccines.

She approached the parking lot and saw two vehicles in the parking area, neither of which looked familiar. But that wasn't surprising, because Bobby had a different vehicle each time they'd met.

Peggy parked the bike and watched as a couple walked toward a car that waited for them. As they approached, the rear doors opened for them. They got in and the car drove off. She followed a path into the park, passing a children's play area and basketball courts. Then she saw a person sitting by themselves on an isolated picnic table away from any other seating or paths.

"Hi, Bobby," she said, as she neared him.

"Peggy. Good to see you, as always." Bobby stood and gave her a friendly hug.

He wore dress pants and a shirt and looked like he was headed to a business meeting. He was average height, and appeared to be of Anglo descent, with a neat mustache and short-cropped hair. There was a crooked scar on his chin, but other than that he was unremarkable. Next to him on the table sat a nylon bag the size of a small backpack.

"I have the photos you wanted." Peggy held out the advanced data drive.

Bobby took the device and pulled a pocket comp from the bag. He placed the data drive next to the comp. Within a couple seconds, the data had been removed from the drive and transferred to a server in a nation with hostile intentions toward the United States. He then pocketed the data drive, but kept the comp in his hand and started pushing buttons to input data.

"Go ahead and check the balance of your account," he said. "You'll see that the agreed amount is now there."

Peggy removed her own pocket comp from her jacket and went to work on it for a few seconds. She saw that the balance in her offshore account had increased by $150,000.

She put the comp back in her pocket. "It's all there. Thank you."

"Peggy, you've done good work, and we've got one final request for you."

This wasn't the first time he'd used the word *we*, and it made her more uncomfortable each time she heard it. Who was *we*? He'd always refused to elaborate when she asked.

"Final request?" she said.

She'd been supplying information every few weeks, in exchange for a nice amount of money. She deposited close to a year's salary each time they'd met. Her only stipulation had been that she wasn't asked to provide anything considered confidential.

"In the lab, there's a vaccine referenced as X-5207. We need you to get a vial of that and bring it to me."

Peggy felt her skin growing cold and her heart rate increasing. She was in trouble and she knew it. All formulas that the lab was working on had a code name. The first letter indicated how hazardous it was. X stood for extreme. Bobby had just asked her for a sample of possibly the most dangerous specimen in the lab.

X-5207 was something that Peggy had heard about. She wasn't aware of what it was because her clearance level didn't allow her to know. She knew it was something that some of the researchers in the lab were spending most of their time on, and it had some people extremely excited. Many of the senior people working on the X-5207 project had occasionally been going off-site for meetings in the last few months.

"I don't have access to that. I can't get to lab specimens. They keep those in the hot area, and I only can go in there for specific cleaning tasks, and I'm always supervised."

"We already have that taken care of. Tomorrow there will be no one working at the Argon lab. I believe there's a major power system upgrade scheduled for 8:00 a.m. The lab will be shut down except for critical systems, which will be on backup power. Even the communications circuits will be offline during this time."

Peggy felt a chill run down her spine from him knowing that information. It was all true—and secret. She'd participated in discussions around planning the outage and the best ways to make sure all systems came back online after the maintenance had completed.

She sat on the picnic table bench. "That is true. However, I can't enter the lab area, especially the hot zone. All lab access is tied to my biochip, and I don't have clearance."

Bobby smiled and nodded. "We're going to give you a new biochip that will allow you access."

"If you replace my biochip, I won't be able to do anything!" I can't make purchases, call a car, or even get into my apartment" Peggy said, the anxiety in her voice increasing.

"Relax. We've got that all taken care of. We aren't removing your current chip. We will provide you with a wide frequency scrambling band that you'll wear over your own biochip to hide its signal."

Peggy paused, letting all the information sink in. "When I agreed to do this, I said I wouldn't provide anything classified. This goes way over that line. I'm not doing it."

Bobby smiled at her again with an amused expression. He took out his pocket comp and held it out for her to see. The screen displayed all the purchases she'd made with the money he'd given her. Purchases she should never have been able to afford. It also showed a record of all of the deposits made into her offshore account and the withdrawals she'd made. The images also included all the information she'd given to Bobby over the last few months, including the pictures she'd provided today.

"Do you have any idea what the courts would do to someone who intentionally took all this information from a secret government-funded lab and turned it over to someone in exchange for money?"

Peggy didn't know the exact answer to that question, but she knew she'd face years of imprisonment. She sat quietly, too stunned to say anything or to even wipe away the tears running down her face.

Finally, she looked up at Bobby and saw him entering data on his comp.

"It still won't work," she said.

"Why not?

"Once they realize the X-5207 is missing, they'll review

computer data and learn that it was me. The false biochip might get me in, but they'll eventually figure it out."

"Very true. Do you remember back when we first met? You told me your dream was to save up enough money so you could retire to the Caribbean and live on a boat."

"I remember."

"Take your comp and look at your account again."

Feeling confused, Peggy took it out and checked her offshore balance. It had increased by $5 million.

"I don't understand. What does this mean?"

"That is $5 million more in your account. When you deliver the X-5207 to me, I'll add an additional $10 million. That will be more than enough for you to retire in the Caribbean. We will also replace your real biochip with one that has a new identity for you."

"So my choices are to get rich and retire, or go to prison?"

"Yes. Those are the two choices." He removed two items from the bag.

One was a syringe containing the new biochip, which was about the size of a grain of rice. The other was a broad band made of elastic cloth mesh.

"Slip this band over your right forearm and the chip in your arm will be unable to communicate. If you need to use your chip, put the band over the left arm where I'm about to inject this new chip. It will allow you access to all areas of the lab."

"How did you get a biochip that has access to the lab?"

"I could tell you, but instead I'll just say that there are some things you're better off not knowing."

Peggy held out her left arm, wondering what the last statement meant, and Bobby inserted the needle.

Chapter Twenty-One

IT WAS STILL DARK OUTSIDE WHEN PEGGY WILSON GOT OUT OF bed. Her virtual assistant was going to wake her in another half-hour, but she hadn't been sleeping and couldn't take staring at the ceiling any longer. She slipped out of bed and headed for the shower. As she bathed, she made sure to keep the transparent mesh band in place on her left arm. Bobby had warned her not to let the new biochip communicate with anything until she was ready for it to.

After showering and dressing, she dug out the largest travel bag she owned and filled it with all the things that mattered the most. She wasn't sure when she'd leave for the Caribbean, but she assumed it would be soon after the meeting where she would turn over the X-5207 to Bobby.

Peggy looked around her cozy apartment. It wasn't very big, but she had grown to like it. Unfortunately after today was over, she wouldn't be able to spend another night there. Either she would be on her way to her dream retirement, or she would be running from lab security and the authorities.

Sitting on the couch, she pulled up a book from her electronic library. It was one she'd purchased several years ago and had information on the Caribbean Islands. She planned to start in St. Thomas and get a boat. She would then spend a few years exploring most of the other islands.

As much as she tried, she couldn't get her mind off her dilemma, and eventually set the pocket comp, that was displaying the book, down. Bobby had done an excellent job of trapping her. She now suspected that all the other information she'd taken for him was meaningless. It was all about getting his hooks into her so she'd have no choice but to agree to get him the sample. As hard as she tried to think of a way out, she didn't believe it was possible. She was going to have to see this through to the end and hope for the best.

After another half-hour of pacing, she left her apartment and hopped on her motorcycle. Usually she took a car to work, but she'd be going directly to see Bobby after she acquired the sample.

It was a warm summer morning in the Arizona desert, and the sun was just coming over the horizon. Peggy started the motorcycle and left the parking lot of her apartment. She pulled onto a road that was already filling with cars taking their riders to work. Stopping at a fast food restaurant, she got a breakfast sandwich and coffee. The coffee cup went in the built-in cup holder, and she enabled the auto-drive. While not fully autonomous, the bike could do most of the work. The GPS knew where she was going, and using the auto-drive also engaged the bike's stability system. The motorcycle wouldn't tip over now, even if she tried to make it. She seldom rode like this, preferring to enjoy having the bike under her control. The one exception was when she ate.

She released the handlebars and the bike took over. She focused on her food, and found the biscuit to be soggy and the ham cold. Even so, she closed her eyes and tried to relax and eat. She opened them again when she heard a beeping sound. The sound was alerting her that the bike would be making a turn. While the bike wouldn't tip over, she could fall off if she wasn't ready for an unexpected maneuver.

When she finished eating, she took back manual control for the last leg of the journey. She'd turned off the highway and was on a narrow dirt road. There were no signs of people for several miles. Just desert and the occasional sign warning against trespassing. Eventually she reached a dilapidated barrier blocking the road. Anyone not knowing better would think it was an abandoned roadblock from fifty or more years ago. When the bike pulled within five feet of it, the sensors hidden in the barrier read the biochip in her forearm, and the whole barrier slid off the road, opening a path for her. At the same time, the electronic security system transmitted a signal to the guards who were about a hundred yards up from the barrier. This informed them that a motorcycle with Peggy Wilson was approaching. Since the rider on the bike had been identified and approved at the gate, the guards just waved at her as she approached and sped past.

She continued another mile up the dirt road until she reached a large storage building that looked to have been abandoned for many years. There was a large empty dirt parking area out front. She dismounted and entered the building. As she passed through the door, a sensor read her biochip, and a section of the wall opened, revealing an elevator that had its doors open and waiting for her. She entered and descended forty feet into the Argon Technologies facility. From what she had heard, this site and some of the existing underground buildings had been part of a nuclear missile silo over a hundred years before.

When the elevator arrived at level 4, Peggy walked down the narrow concrete re-enforced hall and then turned left, toward her workstation.

"Assistant, is the power maintenance still on schedule?"

A small box on her desk replied, "Yes, Miss Wilson. It will begin in four minutes."

"How many other people are in the facility?"

"Only one. Maintenance Chief DeCosta is in his office on level two."

Peggy left her work area and went down another passage that led to the lab. As she walked, most of the hall lights went out, and she heard an automated voice say, "Power disruption detected. Primary systems online. Secondary and non-essential systems unavailable."

Peggy stopped and removed the band from her left arm and covered the biochip in her right arm. She then continued toward the lab, and glanced up at a security camera. The LED light that was always glowing green was now dark. If the cameras had remained powered up, she would never be able to complete her plan.

The doors to the lab opened as she approached. At this she felt a little disappointed. She partially hoped that the new chip wouldn't work. It would be a way out of this mess. She approached the door leading to the dressing room and it, too, opened for her.

A mechanical voice said, "Welcome, Doctor Cox. We're running on backup power only. Most systems are offline."

As Peggy stepped in, the door closed behind her. She stopped and braced herself against the wall. Doctor Elizabeth Cox was a senior researcher at Argon. The chip in her arm had identified her as Cox. The dread that Peggy had been feeling since her meeting with Bobby went through the roof.

Though distracted, Peggy managed to undress and change into one of the six biohazard suits that hung in the room. Normally, getting into a suit was a two-person job. The second person made sure that all the seals were closed so there would be no leaks. She had seen a training video that showed how a single person could don the suit if necessary, but that was against lab procedures.

Once her biohazard suit was on and sealed, she moved to the equipment room. She pulled the hood to the suit up over her head, then strapped on a power belt which had hung on a hook, and plugged in the suit. All the air in the suit was expelled, and the suit, previously baggy, became skin tight. She took a seat on the bench, placed special boots on, and then put on disposable gloves. From another hook, she took a facemask and tightened it around her head, making sure the seal between the mask and hood was airtight. Last, she put on a rigid backpack which contained the pressurized air she would be breathing.

She then left the equipment room and moved into the decontamination room. Grabbed a hose hanging from her backpack, took a final deep breath, and then flipped a switch on the mask to block any outside air from entering. She attached the hose to her mask and purified air began flowing. Since she was moving into the hot zone, the scanners simply made sure that the entry door fully sealed before opening the door into the level 4 biohazard lab. She stepped in and the doors behind her closed, sealing her into the potentially deadly hot zone.

"Hello, Doctor Cox," said the virtual attendant. "We have limited power, and many systems are offline."

Peggy moved to the refrigerated cabinet where the samples were stored. She noticed that most of the equipment on the work surfaces was sitting dark from lack of power. Fortunately refrigeration was critical enough that it still operated.

The intelligence in the cabinets read the biochip and noted that Doctor Elizabeth Cox was authorized to be in there. After searching, Peggy found the three vials marked X-5207 and placed one on the counter next to her. She pressed a button to activate the robotic system that would handle the deadly sample. Nothing happened. Without power, she would have to do this by hand.

She then located an empty glass vial and a large bottle containing sterile saline and an empty glass vial. She took a syringe and withdrew all the contents of the vial marked X-5207, and injected it into the empty vial. Then she used a new syringe to remove saline from the large bottle. This saline went into the now-empty vial marked X-5207, and she returned this marked vial to the cabinet from which it had originally come. Hopefully, replacing the X-5207 with saline wouldn't be discovered before she was out of the country.

She disposed of the syringes according to lab procedure, in a slot on the work surface. It would end up in the incinerator, which was two levels below this one.

Chapter Twenty-Two

PEGGY RETURNED ALL THE EQUIPMENT SHE USED AND THEN double checked to make sure everything was back where it had been when she entered the lab. She took the unmarked vial and pressed the button to open the door to the long decontamination room. Moved into decon, and the door to the hot zone, now behind her, closed. She stepped into an alcove marked *1,* and toxic chemicals sprayed at her from three directions. She slowly turned in circles and the spray covered every inch of her containment suit. The decontamination spray would kill and wash away anything harmful that might have gotten on her protective suit. When the first stage of decontamination was complete, she went to the next station, marked *2.* There, she went through the same procedure all over again, this time with a different cleaning agent. Finally, she went to the spot marked *3,* where it started all over again, this time with water.

Peggy walked to the door and hit a button, indicating that she was ready to leave. Before the door opened, huge exhaust fans engaged, replacing the air in the room. Finally, the light turned green, indicating that she was clear to leave. She took a deep breath and unhooked her air supply, and the door opened. She stepped through and the door closed behind her. After removing the pack, suit, boots, and mask, she placed them in a large bag, sealed it, and dropped into a chute in the wall which would transport the bag for additional cleaning. The gloves went into another chute that led to the incinerator. Once those systems had power, the gloves would be burned, along with the syringes.

She went into one of the shower stalls, where she scrubbed for several minutes using special soap and shampoo. Only after completing each of these steps could she return to the dressing room and put her clothes back on. After dressing, she stuck the unlabeled vial into a pouch strapped around her waist, and as she left the dressing room, the computerized voice said, "Have a good day, Doctor Cox."

She had been trying to push thoughts about Elizabeth Cox from her mind. The two of them weren't friends. They existed at different levels within the company, but they'd enjoyed a few nice conversations over the years. This final comment from the attendant renewed the thoughts about Cox in Peggy's mind.

Peggy took the mesh band from her right arm, placed it on her left, and headed to her workstation.

"Assistant, before today, when was Doctor Elizabeth Cox in the building?"

"She was here two days ago."

"Do you know why she wasn't at work yesterday?"

After a pause, the voice said, "Doctor Cox reported in sick yesterday and said she'd be staying at home."

"Assistant, locate Doctor Cox's address and send it to the nav system on my bike."

"Done."

Peggy headed to the elevator and then noticed it was non-responsive due to lack of power, so she took the emergency stairs up the sixty feet to the surface. She got on her bike and started it up, engaged the auto-drive and selected the destination from the navigational system. As she rode, Peggy kept thinking about the sample on her belt. What was it? What made it so valuable that they would pay over $15 million for it? Who were they, and what would they do with it? How did they get a copy of Doctor Cox's biochip? Was it a copy?

After about twenty minutes, the bike slowed as it entered a subdivision. Peggy took over manual control and followed the navigation system until she reached the address displayed on the bike's console. She recognized the police security drones. Deployed at the edges of the property, they each had a flashing message on their large screen that said, *Do Not Enter Per Police Order. Crime Scene.* Lasers shined between them. If anyone entered the property, the drones would summon the police.

Peggy stopped the bike at the curb and stared at the flashing LEDs on the drones. She dismounted the motorcycle and looked at the house. She had no idea what had happened here, but she knew it was related to the trouble she'd gotten herself into with Bobby.

She heard a car approaching from the direction she'd come. She glanced at it and saw it was just a robocar. She looked again when the car slowed and stopped next to her. The rear window lowered and a middle-aged oriental woman looked out at her.

"Did you know Elizabeth?" the woman said.

"We worked together."

"Such a terrible thing to happen. This is always such a quiet neighborhood."

"All I heard was that something had happened to her. We didn't get any details," Peggy lied, hoping for more information.

"She was murdered in her home. I heard the police saying she'd been chopped up," The woman said, glad for the chance to tell the story.

"When was this?"

"Yesterday morning."

"Thank you." She got on her bike and started the engine.

When the woman's car had moved on, Peggy looped around and headed back the way she'd come. She took manual control and accelerated rapidly. Tears ran down her cheeks as she thought about how she was responsible for this.

"Warning! You're exceeding traffic speed limits," her motorcycle said.

She ignored it. It always felt good to go fast, and right now she was looking for something to make her feel a little better.

When the speed exceeded a hundred miles per hour, "Warning! Your speed is in severe danger range. Decelerate immediately."

Peggy disengaged the safety system and continued her acceleration, navigating several turns as the adrenaline coursed through her body. The excitement and focus needed to drive at that speed took her thoughts away from Doctor Elizabeth Cox. Then the biochip in her left arm popped into her mind and she realized that the dead woman's chip was still inside her. She looked down at her left arm as the horror sunk in.

Peggy returned her focus to the road as an oncoming truck appeared and began passing her. Both vehicles were in their own lanes, but the truck's appearance was sudden because of the speed of the bike. She instinctively turned slightly away from it, and the curb was just inches away. She overcorrected, moving back to the left, and lost control of the bike.

Peggy and the bike separated from one another as they both tumbled end over end across the roadway and onto the grassy shoulder at 115 mph.

As the bones in her body were breaking, so did the glass vial in the pouch strapped to her waist.

Chapter Twenty-Three

DEPUTY SHERIFF LISA KRAMER SAT IN THE FRONT SEAT OF her patrol car. She had parked in the lot of the local high school, under the shade of a large tree. It was over a hundred degrees outside, and even with the air conditioning blowing full force, it was still hot under the noontime sun. There were no other vehicles in the lot today, because it was a Saturday.

Lisa held a tuna wrap in one hand and her pocket comp in the other. She watched an advertisement for a resort in Bermuda. Tomorrow at this time, she'd be flying to that resort with her husband for their honeymoon. They had gotten married two months earlier, but because of work schedules they'd delayed the honeymoon until now.

She'd married Doug after dating him for five years. They'd met in college and had been together ever since. Tomorrow, they would leave to enjoy ten days of sun and sand. And today, all she could think about was Bermuda.

"Tango-six, emergency," said the car's virtual attendant, followed by three loud beeps from the console.

"Go ahead," Lisa replied.

"Approximately 1650 County Highway 12. Motorcycle

accident. Driver possibly unresponsive," the vehicle's mechanical voice informed her.

As Lisa put her lunch away and confirmed that the navigation system had the correct location, the vehicle already had started moving out of the parking lot on its own. She pulled the Y-shaped harness over her head and fastened it to the buckle between her legs, then grabbed the two oversized joysticks on each side of her seat. These controlled the car's steering, acceleration, and breaking. The car was capable of getting her to the accident without her input, but department policy stated that vehicles had to be under human control during emergency driving conditions.

She flipped a switch on the side of the left joystick and the emergency lights lit up and the siren blared, steadily increasing in volume. She shoved the two controls all the way forward, and was pushed back in her seat as the vehicle rapidly accelerated. Her instruments showed her that at her speed of a hundred miles per hour, it would take her a little over three minutes to arrive.

Lisa could feel the sensation as the adrenaline surged through her system and she loved that feeling. It was a part of why she remained in law enforcement. She came out of a turn, and her vehicle, which was in communication with multiple satellites, informed her that she was on a mile-and-a-half straightaway and that there were no other vehicles in her path. She pressed a button on the hand control and increased her speed by fifty miles per hour. She was so focused on driving that she never noticed the console update her with the new arrival time.

After about a minute and a half, the console said, "Approaching scene. Begin decelerating."

Lisa pulled back on the hand controls and decelerated. She could see two robocars pulled to the side of the road. Their occupants were outside, surveying at the carnage. Within a few seconds, she had stopped and was releasing her safety harness. She exited the vehicle and was impressed at how large the debris field was. The first parts of the destroyed bike were by her bumper, and it extended for about a hundred yards down the road. It didn't take an accident investigator to determine that the motorcycle had been going extremely fast.

She saw the driver lying face-up on the grass, just off the road. Her body had taken a severe amount of damage in the crash. As Lisa approached, she was aware of the smell of spilled fuel and heard the crunching of the chunks of debris under her boots. She bent down and took a device from her belt, pressed the end with two metal tips against the victim's forehead, and held it there for fifteen seconds. She stood back up and looked at the readout. There was no brain activity.

Lisa pressed the small device connected to her collar and spoke, "Tango-six."

"Go ahead Tango-six."

"Slow EMS to non-emergency. DOA."

Deputy Kramer returned to the body. There was something wrapped around the driver's left hand. She grabbed it and saw that it was a mesh band. The material was familiar to all law enforcement officers. Bands like this were often used to hide the signal of a biochip for someone who didn't want their identity determined by scanners. It looked to Lisa like it had been on the arm and had been pulled down during the crash.

Lisa took the same scanner she previously used and changed the setting to read biochips, then scanned the body, hoping to identify the young woman. She was more than a little surprised when she got two responses. While it wasn't illegal to mask a biochip's signal, it was suspicious. But using a false biochip was a crime. However, no one would be getting prosecuted in this case.

She looked at the two names on the screen. The first was Peggy Wilson. The name and data that came back about her meant nothing to the deputy. But the second, Elizabeth Cox, did. She'd heard about that case. She was a murder victim, and now it looked like her biochip had been stolen during the attack. This accident call was getting more and more interesting.

The only other thing that caught Lisa's attention was a pouch strapped around the driver's waist. She unzipped the pouch and reached in to get the contents. She was a bit distracted as she did this, thinking about the connection to the murder victim. She felt something wet on her fingers and jerked her hand out, realizing that she should have been more cautious. As she did, a small shard of glass sliced her finger.

Chapter Twenty-Four

LISA KRAMER ROLLED OVER IN THE BED. HER HUSBAND, Doug, had just silenced the virtual attendant, which had awakened them, as scheduled. Usually she'd have been up extra early, excited to leave on her trip to Bermuda. But today she just wanted to roll over and go back to sleep. Her head pounded and she thought she might even have a mild fever.

She waited until she heard Doug get out of the shower, and then forced herself to get up. She felt dizzy at first, but that cleared almost right away. The new bride swallowed some cold and fever medication with a handful of water she scooped from the bathroom sink. Then to make sure she didn't forget, Lisa put the rest of the pills into her carry-on bag before getting in the shower.

After drying off, she removed and disposed the wet bandage covering the slice she'd gotten on her finger the previous day. She decided that maybe she felt a little better, and forced herself to get moving. There was no way she'd let a minor illness ruin her honeymoon plans. She dressed in a casual outfit that would be comfortable for traveling, and found that Doug already had her luggage by the door and held a cup of coffee for her as she came downstairs.

"Honey, are you feeling all right?" he said. "You're looking a little rough."

"I think I'm coming down with something. I took some meds. Don't worry. This won't interfere with our trip."

"Okay, let me know if there's anything I can do."

"I'll try to get some sleep on the plane, and then hopefully I'll be feeling better."

At 7:00 a.m., a car pulled up to the curb in front of their modest house located in a middle-class subdivision. The couple exited their home and approached the open rear door of the vehicle, which had opened for them.

A computerized voice from inside the car said, "I'm here for Lisa and Doug Kramer."

"That is us," Doug said. "Please open the trunk."

As the trunk opened, Lisa got in the car, and Doug loaded the luggage before getting in. As they entered, the vehicle scanned them, and their identities were confirmed, and payment information received.

"Has your destination changed, Mr. Kramer?"

"No. Airport."

Doug put his arm around his new wife and held and comforted the sick woman. As he did so, he repeatedly inhaled some of the air she exhaled. He never suspected that within four days, he would be dead. Ironically, Lisa Kramer, who would eventually be known as patient zero, the first person infected, would be one of the 16 percent of the infected that would survive.

Lisa slept for the forty-minute drive to the airport. When they arrived, she felt worse but forced herself to move on. All the ticketing and boarding pass information was scanned directly from their biochips. There was a small electronic tag in each piece of their luggage which linked the baggage directly to the owner. The airline would scan each bag and the owner's intended destination, contact information, address, and current location would be made available.

Doug placed each piece of luggage on a conveyor belt and watched as it was whisked away, hopefully, to meet them at their destination. Security was slow that day, and each passenger waited for their turn to walk through the scanner array. The people bunched up, they all got quite close to each other, during the process, and over twenty people passed within three feet of Lisa.

As soon as the couple was cleared through security, they proceeded to the gate, where an agent scanned them again to verify that they were in the correct area. In just the short time they were in their local airport, Lisa managed to infect twelve airport employees and fifty-six passengers. There were also four people that would become infected while riding in the robocar that had transported the Kramers that morning.

Of the twelve infected airport employees, nine of them would make it to work tomorrow, where they would infect six hundred and seventy-four other passengers who would carry the X-5207 infection even further. However, that wasn't the most significant problem.

Lisa and Doug had a two-hour layover in Atlanta before their flight to Bermuda. Lisa tried to sleep, but was restless. Eventually she couldn't stand sitting any longer and stood.

"Where are you going?" Doug said.

"I just need to stretch my legs. I hope moving around a little will help."

"Do you want me to go with you?"

"No, I'm okay. I'll be back in a few minutes."

"Okay, don't be too long. You need to save your strength."

Lisa walked away from the boarding area and down the concourse. There was a large crowd gathered by the neighboring gate. There was a plane just starting to board, and this crowd would be on the next flight leaving from this gate. Those assembled were waiting for the seats in the boarding area to become available.

As Lisa passed through the crowd, she overheard some

kids discussing how they were headed to a major amusement park and would get to be on the rides until late tonight. They were excited and were discussing everything they wanted to do while there. Little did the kids know that their presence in that park, now that they were infected, would significantly contribute to accelerating the spread of the disease.

After making it through the crowd, Lisa stopped in a shop, went to the cooler and withdrew two bottles of water. She now was now exhausted and wanted to rest again. She headed out the door, where a scanner read her biochip and took her payment for the water.

During her time in Atlanta, Lisa infected 362 people. Other than those headed to the amusement park, she also encountered many who were traveling internationally. While the infected wouldn't become contagious for twelve hours, many of them were traveling for work and would be returning through Atlanta and other hubs.

One of the key accomplishments of Argon Technologies was shrinking the period between becoming infected and contagious. They had succeeded quite well.

In three days, X-5207 infections had broken out in eighteen countries. And within a week, there were only four nations that didn't have any documented cases of the disease.

Chapter Twenty-Five

THE JETLINER LANDED AT WADE INTERNATIONAL AIRPORT IN St. George's Parish on the island of Bermuda. For most of the two hundred and thirty people on the plane, the trip seemed uneventful. Little did they know that while they sat in their seats, they were being attacked at the microscopic level and a death sentence had been delivered to all but forty-two of them. Other than the two members of the flight crew, assigned to the rear of the aircraft, only seven other people even noticed that there was something wrong with the woman in seat 31D.

Lisa slept for most of the trip, not even awakening for drink service. When the aircraft landed, Doug helped her to her feet and carried her bag as she exited the plane under her own power. When they got to baggage claim, she sat, too tired to stand, while Doug waited to hear their names called.

"Doug and Lisa Kramer, bay 94," the system announced, and Doug walked over to a row of luggage bays.

They reminded him of oversized high school lockers. He went to the bay with his number to collect their bags. Each set of luggage was enclosed in a steel cage that came up from the floor and into the numbered bay. The steel cage remained closed until Doug's biochip was detected. All around him, others were collecting their bags as they rose into place. Names and bay numbers were being announced by the system every few seconds, in a variety of languages based on the preference on the airline reservation.

Doug pulled their bags out, and as soon as the door shut, the cage descended into the floor. By the time he'd gotten back to Lisa, another set of luggage had appeared in slot 94, and another name was announced, this time in German.

Doug was so preoccupied that he didn't notice the announcement of the luggage bay that was previously his. Instead, he was focused on his new bride. He had known Lisa for many years and had seen her sick several times, but never like this. Sweat soaked her body, and she was deathly pale. During the flight, she had developed a deep, rattling cough. And she seemed to be focusing hard on keeping herself upright on the bench.

"Babe, are you OK?"

"Sure." Lisa answered, getting unsteadily to her feet.

"I think we should take you to a hospital. You're getting worse."

"No." She answered adamantly. Just get me to the resort. A little sleep by the pool, and I'll be feeling better."

Doug reluctantly agreed. He might have pushed harder for the hospital, but he wanted to rest, too. He'd had a headache since getting off the plane and he felt exhausted.

Helping her to the taxi waiting area while pulling their luggage was a challenge for him. They only waited a few minutes for a cab, and Doug was surprised to see that it was a much older vehicle. There was even a driver for the car, who assisted them with their bags, and Doug helped Lisa get into the backseat for the twenty-minute trip to the resort. On the way, Doug held his wife and watched the driver. The last time he'd been in a car with a driver, he was a child. It was interesting to watch someone operating the vehicle.

"Welcome to Bermuda. My name is Abnon. Are you coming in from the United States?" The driver asked.

"Yes, from the U.S.," Doug replied, hoping the driver wouldn't be overly chatty.

"Is this your first time here?"

"Yes. We're here on our honeymoon."

"Oh, honeymoon. Congratulations. It looks like flying does not agree with your new bride."

"Thank you. No, she's not feeling very well."

"I am sure that with some sun and fun, she will be back to herself in no time."

"I hope so."

Doug relaxed as the talking stopped for a few minutes.

Unfortunately, it resumed when they entered a highway.

"Most people from the States find it strange to see me driving. You no longer have any cars with drivers, right?"

"That is true. Cars with drivers are very uncommon in the U.S."

"We have been slowly switching over. We are about ten to fifteen years behind you. About seventy-five percent of the cars here are fully automated. Or what you call, robocars. Soon, I will need to find a new job."

Doug didn't want to be rude, but he also didn't want to talk anymore, so he stayed silent and just held his sick wife.

When their driver dropped them off, they entered the ornate lobby, which was extremely crowded. Many people were still checking out, and even more waiting to check-in. Fortunately the check-in process moved along quickly. As soon as Lisa and Doug approached the counter, their biochips were scanned.

A computerized voice said, "Welcome Mr. and Mrs. Kramer. Please present your pocket comps."

Doug pulled his out and looked at Lisa.

She shook her head. "Later," she said, in a weak tone.

Doug held his out, and the computerized voice said,

"Thank you. Directions to your room, along with a listing of all activities and amenities, have been sent to your pocket comp. From there, you will have access to lookup or reserve anything within the property. You are in Room B16, and the door lock has been synced to your biochip. Do you have any questions?"

"Do you have an onsite physician?" Doug said.

"Yes, there is a physician on duty twenty-four hours a day. Do you need to see her?"

Lisa replied, "No, that's not necessary."

The stubbornness was a trait Doug usually appreciated about his wife, but not today.

Looking at the pocket comp, he guided them across the lobby and to a path that would take them past the main pool and to their building. While they were in the crowded lobby, they passed within twenty feet of sixty-two people. Not overly close, but close enough, now that the cough had developed.

They were outside on the upper level at the back of the lobby. From there, they could look over much of the resort, and the view was amazing. Magnificent palm trees and several beautiful swimming pools were visible, with the Atlantic Ocean in the background. Doug had seen that view in the online brochure, but it was nothing compared to being there.

"Look. Isn't it amazing?" he said.

"Uh-huh," Lisa replied, not interested in the majestic view.

Doug was impressed with his wife. He didn't think she would make it all the way to the room, but she kept going. The door opened as they approached, and he assisted her inside, knowing their luggage would be along shortly. He led her over to the bed and helped her sit.

"Do you want to rest here, or at the pool?" he said.

"Here," Lisa replied, with a weak voice.

"Earlier, you said you wanted to rest by the pool."

"Here."

"Okay. I'll get you tucked in."

"Thank you. I'm sorry. I just feel so bad."

"I know. You sleep. I might go get something to eat."

"Good. I love you."

"I love you, too. Do you want me to bring you back something to eat?"

"I guess, something small and a drink," Lisa replied, knowing that she hadn't had anything to eat today.

"Okay, I will. Now get some rest."

Chapter Twenty-Six

DOUG WATCHED HIS WIFE AS SHE SLEPT AND WANTED TO STAY in the room so he could be there if she needed anything. He even considered ordering room service. But he knew that would be noisy and she might not get the sleep that she needed.

So the new groom left the room and headed to the main restaurant. The buffet was supposed to be open for another hour and a half. Walking across the grounds, Doug was concerned because he felt a bit chilled and more tired, too. After lunch, he would join Lisa for a nap.

He entered the restaurant and got in line with dozens of other vacationers, not realizing that the incubation period had progressed to the point where he too was contagious. Doug looked at all the food on the expansive buffet and was impressed with the variety and quantity. Any other time he would have loved the opportunity to sample many of the options, but today none of it appealed to him. In the end, his plate remained empty except for a few pieces of tropical fruit.

He sat outside on a reclining pool chair and ate, feeling disappointed because it seemed as if there was no taste to the food. He looked around the beautiful resort and at all the people having a good time, and all he wanted to do was take a nap. Without even realizing it, he drifted off to sleep, waking two hours later. He stood, left his plate on the table by his pool chair, and headed back to their room, feeling worse than before. Halfway back, he realized he'd completely forgotten to bring back something for his bride.

When Doug approached the room, the door opened for him, and as he stepped over the threshold, he heard his new wife's raspy, labored breathing. He walked to the bed and saw Lisa lying on her back and looking even paler than before. Her breathing was labored and it sounded like there might be fluid in her lungs.

"Lisa, wake up!" He shook her shoulder.

She didn't respond.

Doug could feel the panic building and tried to force it down. "Attendant, medical emergency. I need an ambulance, now!"

After a brief pause, the electronic voice said, "Medical response team is on the way."

In just a couple minutes, three people came rushing into the room. The first had a uniform and a nametag that identified him as resort security. Another man followed him, and he carried two large bags. His nametag identified him as a paramedic assigned to the resort. The third person was a tall, slender woman with Arabic features. She appeared to be in her mid-forties.

She spoke first, "I am Doctor Krahan. What happened?"

"My wife has been sick all day. She seemed to be steadily getting worse. She just wanted to sleep after we checked in, and now she won't wake up."

As the doctor continued asking questions, the paramedic took a sealed package containing two disk-shaped devices from his bag. Each was about an inch and a half in diameter. He removed an adhesive strip from the back of each and attached one to Lisa's chest and one to her forehead. LED lights started blinking on each for several seconds. Then a beep sounded, and now there was only a single green light on each, and they were blinking in unison, which signaled that the devices were communicating with each other. The medic took a twelve-inch digital screen from his bag and activated it. When the data from the attached devices started coming in, he moved closer to the doctor and held the screen so they could both see it.

The two medical providers glanced at each other, an unspoken message communicated.

Doctor Krahan touched a device at her collar and said, "Inform the ambulance Code One medical emergency." She looked at Doug. "Sir, your wife is very sick. Her vital signs are unstable. Is there any more about her illness that you can tell me?"

Doug shook his head, "I don't think so. It all started this morning when she woke up. She just keeps getting worse." As he said this, he felt dizzy and had to sit on the corner of the bed.

"Mr. Kramer." Doctor Krahan said when she noticed Doug's apparent weakness and pallor. "Are you sick, too?"

"I think so. It just came on in the last few hours or so. I'm weak, chilled, achy, and want to sleep."

The medic took a box-shaped device with a mask attached and strapped it to Lisa's face. He switched it on, and again picked up the display screen and started entering commands. The device on her face started humming and sealed itself around her mouth and nose. It began filtering most of the nitrogen, carbon dioxide, and other gasses from the air, leaving primarily oxygen, which it pushed in with each breath Lisa took. Because of the settings he made on the control screen, she was now breathing 75 percent oxygen, compared to the normal 21 percent that was in the normal room air. The minor increase in pressure also caused her breaths to be

deeper, and worked to push out the fluids that were accumu-
lating in her lungs.

As Lisa's oxygen levels were coming up, an IV was started
and fluids administered to combat dehydration that was
setting in.

"Mike, hand me another set of transponders, please," said
Dr. Krahan.

The paramedic looked at the doctor as he fished another
set from the bag, and noticed that she was examining the
woman's husband. Soon, he too had the devices on his head
and chest, which were sending their data to the medic's
screen.

The doctor looked up from the screen. "Mr. Kramer,
you're sick, too. You will both need to be admitted to King
Edward VII Memorial Hospital."

"How bad is it?" Doug said.

"We will need to do some tests. But you will both need to
be hospitalized for a few days, at least."

"We're on our honeymoon. This was supposed to be a
great time."

"I am very sorry about that." She pulled a mask from the
medical bag by her feet. "Please put this on."

Doug took the mask and looked at it, confusion evident on
his face.

"It's just until we determine if you're contagious."

He nodded and put the mask on.

"Doctor Krahan," said the room's virtual attendant, "the
ambulance is arriving."

"Understood. Inform them that there are two patients.
One ambulatory and one not."

"Message sent."

Doctor Krahan's decision to put a mask on her patients
kept them from infecting the hospital staff upon admission.
But over twelve hundred patients would walk into the hospital

for treatment of X-5207 symptoms, over the next five days, which allowed the infection to overrun the facility.

The masks did nothing for the three people who'd responded to the Kramers' suite. The imminent deaths of Mike the paramedic and Dr. Krahan were already determined. The security officer who assisted them would spend the next forty years wondering why he'd never gotten sick when almost everyone else did.

Chapter Twenty-Seven

ONE WEEK LATER

LISA KRAMER OPENED HER EYES. THE ROOM LIGHTS WERE bright and painful. Her head hurt, and her gown was wet from sweat. She recognized the container of IV fluid above the bed and could feel where the catheter entered her forearm. The oxygen mask irritated her face, so she removed it. That simple act tired her, and she closed her eyes to rest.

The next time she opened them, she saw an elderly woman with a mask covering her face, looking down at her. The oxygen mask was back on Lisa's face. The woman held an electronic screen and focused on the readings it displayed.

"Please leave it off.," Lisa said as she reached for the oxygen mask, her voice dry and raspy.

"Oh, you're awake. That's exciting! How do you feel?"

Lisa could tell that the voice belonged to an elderly woman.

"Very tired and thirsty. Can I have some water?"

The woman had a thoughtful expression. "I think so. I really should ask a doctor or nurse, but that isn't so easy."

"Aren't you my nurse?"

"Me? No. I was a nurse here, but I retired almost twenty years ago. I just came to volunteer when things got so busy.

You can call me Maggie. I think your nurse got sick. I'm not sure if you have one right now."

As Maggie talked, Lisa became aware that she was in a crowded room. It looked to be a four-person room, but there were easily twice as many packed in here. Some people were in beds, and others on portable stretchers.

"I don't understand. What's going on? How long have I been here? Where is my husband, Doug?"

Maggie was confused for a minute. Then she realized Lisa wasn't aware of what had been going on. With sadness evident in her voice, she told her the horrible news, "There's a terrible disease sweeping the island. It sounds like it is in many other places in the world as well. There have been thousands sick, just here on the island. Most of the hospital staff is sick, many dead. The hospital is functioning on volunteers. I believe you were one of the first ones brought in sick. Your chart says that you have been here for about a week. You are lucky to have survived. Actually, I believe you are the first one that has improved this much. Almost no one survives."

"That's horrible. I can't believe I've been sleeping through all that. Has it realty been a week that I've been here?"

"That is what your chart says."

"Doug. That's my husband. Is he sick?" Lisa was terrified to hear the answer.

"I have been working here for three days and I haven't heard anything about him. I will check for you."

When Lisa awoke again, another twelve hours had passed. She pressed her call light and waited over fifteen minutes, before a tall thin man walked in. He, too, wore a mask that hid his facial features.

"Hello, Missus Kramer. I'm Andrew. I am a local pastor that has come in to help where I can."

Lisa nodded. "Do you know anything about my husband? Is he sick?"

"Your husband did get sick. He was admitted at the same

time you were. The two of you were the first cases of this terrible illness. I'm very sorry, but he passed away four days ago."

Lisa began crying hysterically. Andrew took her hand and didn't say anything. He knew it was far too early for words to be of any comfort. This pastor understood how people respond to such news. He had become something of an expert, having given similar news hundreds of times in the last few days.

Because of her weakened condition, Lisa soon cried herself back to sleep. It would be several more hours before she would again face the tragedy and despair her world had fallen into.

It took three more days before she was able to get out of bed on her own. By then, there was almost no non-military air traffic, as nations were trying to control the spread of the disease. Because of this, she found it impossible to get transportation back to the United States.

For the next week, she stayed at the now nearly vacant resort and worked as a volunteer at the hospital. Since she was no longer at risk of contracting the disease, she didn't need the masks that all other non-infected wore.

All hospitals were sharing any information about fighting the disease, and one afternoon Lisa was summoned to take a phone call.

"This is Lisa."

"Lisa, this is Courtney Chelton. I am with the CDC in Atlanta."

"OK. What can I do for you?"

Lisa was exhausted. Her strength was still returning, and she'd been working in the hospital for the last fourteen hours.

"We are working on trying to understand the origins of this outbreak. We have asked all hospitals to let us know when they saw their first sick patients. From the information we have from the King Edward Hospital, you and your husband were possibly the first documented cases of the illness. You were admitted about nine hours before the next patient. That patient was an airport worker in Arizona, at the airport you flew out of. The fact that you were the first documented case, and oddly, also a survivor, makes you very interesting to us. We want to send you several electronic questionnaires to fill out. We would also like you to have some blood drawn. Somehow we're going to have to get that blood back here to test. It's possible that it could provide some needed answers."

"Miss Chelton, I'm more than willing to cooperate. But I am stranded on this island, and I can't get any information about when I can go home. You get me back to the US, and I will give you blood and fill out your questionnaires."

"That's not something I can authorize. But we really need this information. It could help save lives."

"As soon as I'm back in the U.S. You know where to find me. Have a good day."

Lisa disconnected the call and hoped she hadn't been too harsh. She genuinely wanted to help, but she needed to get off this island. Hopefully this would make that happen. She understood that whatever illness she'd woke up with just before leaving on her trip was the cause of all this, and she wanted answers.

Two days later, Lisa boarded a small U.S. Air Force transport aircraft and was headed back to the States. Her honeymoon had been a disaster, and her husband was dead and she didn't even have a body to bury.

Chapter Twenty-Eight

PRESIDENT ABBY RUSSELL WALKED INTO THE SITUATION ROOM in the basement of the West Wing of the White House. As she entered, everyone in the room stood. She took her seat at the head of the table, with the Presidential Seal on the wall behind her.

"Please be seated," she said.

A White House steward placed a cup of coffee in front of her. It was four in the morning, and she'd just vacated this seat five hours earlier. Since the crisis had started, she'd spent much of her time in this room. For the last three days, it had been the same haggard-looking people in here with her. The White House was on lockdown. No one was coming or going, as they hoped to keep the epidemic out of the building.

Around the table sat the Assistant Director of Homeland Security, the National Security Advisor, the Chief of Staff, and the Chairman of the Joint Chiefs. Also seated with them was Joan Marshall, who was employed by the Center for Disease Control (CDC) in Atlanta. The CDC had assigned her to be the White House liaison for the duration of the crisis. She had arrived just before the lockdown went into effect.

On the bank of monitors at the opposite end of the table from the President were four people on the screens. They had remotely connected to the meeting. The first was Kobe Richards, Director of Homeland Security. He was unable to get to the White House before the lockdown. Also on a screen was General Dwain Peck, Director of the United States Army Medical Research Institute of Infectious Diseases (USAM-RID) located at Fort Detrick, Maryland. The last two screens were occupied by Dr. Evelyn Baxter, Director of the CDC, and the final person was new to these meetings and appeared to be nervous.

"What's the current status?" said President Russell.

"Not much change," replied the CDC head.

As the CDC Director, Dr. Evelyn Baker, a tall, thin African-American woman, was always confident and well poised. She was usually the smartest person in the room, and everyone knew it. Today, on the video screen, she looked haggard and defeated.

"The outbreak is still spreading like wildfire," she said. "It has now officially been recognized as a global pandemic. We're in day ten since the first case was reported. Just recapping, that was an American citizen vacationing in Bermuda. It sounds like she became infected before traveling, and she's still alive and improving. We will be evacuating her from the island today and taking her for examination. Right now we are looking at her as patient zero. Interestingly enough, she is also one of the few to survive. We hope to learn something by studying her.

The illness is running rampant in all nations, and nothing so far has had any effect. We're getting some better data in, and it looks like the thing is a synthetic, or man-made pathogen. It appears that roughly 15 percent of the population have some natural immunity and aren't at risk. We're looking into that. It's possible that it could help lead us to a cure. Also, about 16 percent of the infected seem to overcome it on their own. The rest don't survive."

The President shook her head. "We need to figure something out. We need to get ahead of this."

"It's moving much too fast," said Evelyn Baker. "Without some kind of break, we aren't going to get ahead of it."

The room got quiet for a few seconds as the CDC director's ominous news sank in.

"I assume that since we're here at this early hour, there's something new?" the President said.

"Yes, Madam President, there is," replied General Peck of USAMRIID. "We have finally identified what we're dealing with, and we know where it came from."

This generated excitement around the table and on the view screens.

After a few seconds, "Quiet!" said the President. "Let the general speak."

"Thank you, Madam President. The epidemic was caused by what's known as X-5207. It is an experimental synthetic weaponized biotoxin. And this is the disturbing part—it's ours."

The pandemonium erupted again, with everyone yelling out questions. This time, General Peck who yelled across his conference line to get everyone to settle down.

"General, are you saying that this is something your team at Fort Detrick is responsible for?" the President growled.

"No ma'am, not at all. By ours, I mean that it originated in the U.S. On the call with us is Doctor Jake Dexter. He's the director of Argon Technologies. His lab is where X-5207 originated."

"Doctor Dexter, exactly what is it that your company does?" the President said, anger still apparent in her voice.

"Madam President, we were contracted by the U.S. government to research synthetic bio pathogens."

"Specify. What part of the U.S. government are you working for?" The President asked.

"Ma'am, that information is classified."

Leaping to her feet, the President yelled at the screen, "It isn't classified from the President and the National Security Council!"

"No, ma'am, I guess it isn't." Dr. Jake Dexter took a deep breath. "We were contracted by the Defense Department to work on synthetic bio pathogens. It's a black project. I doubt anyone in the room with you knows about it."

The President glared at the Chairman of the Joint Chiefs, Marcus Quimby, who shook his head and gave a faint shrug.

The USAMRIID Director, General Peck, said, "So Argon Technologies is doing off-the-books work for DOD and is weaponizing synthetic bio-pathogens, even though this is against international law?"

There was a long pause.

"Yes, that's what we're doing," Dr. Jake Dexter finally admitted.

"What was the intended use case for this X-5207?" said the National Security Advisor.

"The idea was that it could be used against an enemy population to decimate them and remove their ability to fight. It was all experimental. To the best of my knowledge, there was no plan actually to use it. Just to have as a possible option."

There was another pause.

Then the CDC director said, "How did your experiment get loose?"

"Eleven days ago, there was a partial power shutdown at our facility for maintenance. A lab worker took advantage of the situation. There was almost no one onsite, and many security systems were down. She accessed the lab and stole a vial of X-5207. She did a good job hiding her tracks, and I'm not sure how long it would have taken for us to notice the theft.

But when we began hearing more and more about the outbreak and how the symptoms mirrored what we saw in the lab on computer models, I ordered a complete inspection of every sample of X-5207. That's when we found that the contents of one vial had been replaced with saline, and we realized the outbreak started with our sample. Please keep in mind that this was never supposed to get out of a laboratory environment. It was for testing and research only."

"So how does this connect to patient zero?" the President said.

Joan Marshall, the CDC-White House liaison, spoke up for the first time. "Ma'am, we've connected those dots. Patient zero, who's hospitalized in Bermuda, is a police officer in Arizona, just two towns away from the Argon lab. The person who stole the sample died in some kind of traffic accident shortly after the theft of the bioweapon. Patient zero was the responding officer to that accident. We're making the logical assumption that she became infected at that time."

There was a long pause as everyone digested the information, and then the president said, "Doctor Dexter, you created the world's most deadly bio-weapon and never thought to create an antidote or vaccine?

"No, ma'am, that isn't true. We have a vaccine."

The entire room became silent.

"There's already a vaccine, and we're just hearing about this!" said the Director of Homeland Security shouted.

Defensively Dr. Dexter replied, "We just completed our audit of X-5207 a couple hours ago. We only just learned that the outbreak originated from here."

"How many doses of the vaccine are there?" someone asked.

"There are now eight hundred doses available. There's a military aircraft landing in the next few minutes to transport them to CDC. I've also sent all the information about how the vaccine is produced, to the CDC, and hopefully we can send it to every pharmaceutical company on the planet."

"Doctor Dexter, you say that there are eight hundred doses available," said the CDC Director. "Is that all you've produced?"

"No. There were a thousand doses. We immediately vaccinated what's left of our staff, and they're all at home vaccinating their uninfected family members. As soon as that's done, they'll be returning here so we can work on producing more. We don't have mass production capability, but every dose will help."

"Doctor Dexter, you shouldn't have done that. Every dose should have been turned over. There needs to be a decision-making process as to who gets the first doses," said Kobe Richards, Director of Homeland Security.

"Sir, I'll apologize for many things, but not that. Part of the agreement with my staff when they were sent home with the vaccine, was that they return immediately to begin work on creating more."

"Enough. That's done," the President said. "We will do everything to get as much of the vaccine produced as possible and to share the formula for the vaccine with our allies. We will have further discussion about sharing it with all nations, but that discussion will be with the National Security Council only. Right now I need to know something from Doctor Dexter. We have a vaccine for those that aren't already sick. Is there a treatment strategy or cure for those that are already infected?"

"I'm sorry, Madam President, but there isn't. Just the vaccine for those that are not yet infected. We were just starting on a treatment. That is still a year or more away. "

Chapter Twenty-Nine

FIVE DAYS LATER

IT WAS AGAIN EARLY IN THE MORNING, AND THE SAME GROUP had gathered again around the long table in the White House's John F. Kennedy Conference Room, more commonly known as the Situation Room. Everyone here had received the vaccination against X-5207, but there wasn't yet enough vaccine for the rest of the White House staff, so the Secret Service still strongly regulated who was allowed entrance. No one who hadn't been vaccinated and then gone twenty-four hours without symptoms was permitted to come in. Everyone who entered the building had to first pass through a diagnostic scanner that checked body temperature and other factors. Anything out of a normal baseline got them diverted to a triage area that had been set up on the White House grounds.

"Where do things stand this morning?" said President Abby Russell.

CDC Director, Dr. Evelyn Baker, replied. "As far as the outbreak is concerned, we're now estimating close to two billion people dead and another four billion sick. That's roughly half the world's population, and it's still spreading. Every pharmaceutical company in the U.S. is working on replicating the vaccine, but production is going slowly. Many of the pharmaceutical companies are having difficulty getting staff. They've lost people to the outbreak, and those that are still healthy don't want to go near anyone who might be infected, so they aren't showing up to work. The pharmaceutical companies are offering their staff the first batch of the vaccine in order to get them to come to work. However, production is still very slow. Most of our allies are reporting similar problems."

"Speaking of allies," said General Marcus Quimby, Chairman of the Joint Chiefs, "We're quickly running out of them. As news has spread that this pandemic originated at a U.S. government-funded site, we've become an international pariah. There are protests at almost every foreign military installation. Many nations, as you know, are demanding we remove all U.S. service personnel. These nations want to calm the near riotous crowds that are forming. There have even been incursions onto U.S. bases, and there have been fatalities. We're preparing evacuation plans for every military base outside the continental U.S. so we can quickly pull our personnel if it comes to that."

The President nodded, absorbing the news, "What else?"

"One more thing, ma'am," said the Chairman of the Joint Chiefs. "After discussing this, the Secretary of the Navy has ordered all ships that haven't been in port since this outbreak began to remain at sea. Those crews are all healthy. Until we can get enough vaccine to them to treat the entire crew, we don't want to take the chance of them becoming infected."

"Good call," the President said. "Next?"

The Secretary of State spoke from the leftmost monitor. He'd been traveling internationally at the time of the outbreak and had just returned to the U.S. He still hadn't been medically cleared to enter the White House.

"The decision to not immediately release the vaccine to our non-allies is proving costly. The forty-eight-hour delay in releasing the vaccine formula globally has created rage. Many nations are demanding that we clear out our embassies. There are riots at many locations, and angry mobs have overrun several of our facilities. We have three embassies that are either burning or have already been burned out. I strongly recommend that we evacuate all Foreign Service personnel where there's any civil disobedience, until this all passes."

"Do it," said President Russell. "Evacuate at the first sign of trouble. Same for military installations overseas. I don't want our forces to engage protesters or rioters except as necessary to defend themselves." As she spoke, she felt the heaviness in her chest again.

She'd experienced it several times in the last few days, but it always went away in twenty to thirty minutes. She didn't have time for all the medical evaluations that would come if she mentioned this, so she told no one. This was a crisis and she needed to be healthy. Her country needed to see her strong and in control.

"Along those lines," said the Director of Homeland Security, "I think it is time to recall the bulk of our overseas military personnel. We also have violent protests breaking out here at home. We will need to protect the medical teams who are trying to immunize people. We need to have the manpower and the show of force to maintain law and order. This crisis has already overwhelmed local law enforcement in many areas."

"We can't do that without violating the Posse Comitatus Act," said the National Security Advisor. "The act prohibits U.S. military forces from being used as law enforcement within the U.S."

"Not true," the Attorney General said, from another monitor. "First, the Posse Comitatus Act can be suspended if Congress agrees. Also, the Insurrection Act of 1807 was updated in 2006, and again in 2072, to allow for the use of military personnel on U.S. soil in just this kind of scenario. There's no constitutional or legal reason why we can't use military forces to maintain order for the duration of the crisis."

The Director of Homeland Security nodded. "That's the way I see it, too. We need those troops here to maintain order and to try to assist in vaccine distribution."

The President nodded. "Start bringing our troops home, as appropriate."

"Madam President, there are a couple things I must bring up," said Michael Beltman, Head of the Secret Service.

"Go ahead, Mike." The President sounded lethargic.

"The crowds that are gathering outside the White House and the Capitol Building are growing and becoming more raucous. I think we may soon need to think about getting you to a more secure location. Also, I just got word from the VP's protective detail. The Vice President is ill. He's now in quarantine at Walter Reed National Medical Center. Early indications are that it is X-5207. He was just vaccinated last night. The thought is that he was infected before he was vaccinated."

As more and more horrific news was reported, the President became increasingly despondent. Soon, she was only nodding, and silent.

Chapter Thirty

SIX DAYS LATER

The ultra-modern aircraft known as Air Force One landed at an undisclosed military installation in the central U.S. There was a delay in their departure because the co-pilot, who was on standby to fly, went home sick.

As the evacuation of the President and her family from the White House completed, gunshots echoed. Agents carrying advanced energy rifles surrounded them as they hurried to the aircraft that would get them to safety. The reports they heard from the Secret Service said that there were multiple breaches in the fence surrounding the property. They'd gotten out just in time.

Upon exiting Air Force One, the President and her advisors boarded armored vehicles that whisked them a hundred fifty yards to a re-enforced complex that would serve as a temporary command center. Other agents took the President's family to a housing area that had been cleared out for the First Family.

President Abby Russell had her daily live broadcast to the nation coming up in just twenty minutes. She'd begun holding these since the magnitude of the crisis became known. As they entered the large conference room, there were preparations still underway. The installation of telecommunications equipment was just being completed, and additional seating continued to be setup.

All work stopped, and the workers stood at attention as the exhausted President entered the room. "Please continue," she said.

Everyone noticed how quiet and tired her voice was.

The President took a seat at the table and her aides joined her. They'd been keeping up on developments during the flight.

"What's new?" she said. "What's happening in DC?"

Her Chief of Staff replied, "The rioters have entered the White House, and there are reports of fires. Same with the Capitol. Military and law enforcement are using deadly force to break up the rioters, but that's only so effective."

President Russell started to speak and then hesitated as she felt the chest pain return. She caught herself and continued.

"Congress was supposed to be meeting. They were going to try to meet today to discuss my appointment of Senator Willard as the new Vice President. Did everyone get out of the Capitol before the rioters got in?"

"Not sure, ma'am. There's too much confusion right now to get specifics."

"With over half of both houses of Congress gone from the illness, those that could were going to try to be there for the discussion. We can't continue to lose so much of our leadership."

"I agree, ma'am. We're facing a true continuity of government crisis. Of the twenty successors to the President, we know that twelve are dead, and we can only locate three of the rest right now. And they're cabinet members who are far down the line."

"OK, we can come back to that. Where are we with getting immunizations out to the people? The President asked.

The Director of Homeland Security replied, "The latest

report from the CDC says that most U.S. Pharmaceutical companies are doing everything they can to produce the serum. So far, Stoffer Medical Enterprises has been the most successful. You know Brian Stoffer—he's personally overseeing the operations and has gotten production moving. The problem is there's no good method to get it out to people. Most interstate commerce has stopped. No one wants to be away from home, so trucks aren't moving. We're trying to use the military to help. We've gotten many of the troops immunized, and from there, hospital staff and first responders are high priorities. We're focusing on those that are trying to keep things working. Those that are rioting and in prison are at the end of the list."

The President nodded. "At least we're making some progress. We saw Washington collapse. What about throughout the rest of the country?

"People continue to get sick. There are widespread power and Internet outages. There are just not enough people showing up to work to keep the lights on. Fuel is scarce everywhere. And then there's also the problem with the dead. There are dead people everywhere, and since they're obviously infected, no one wants to go near them, so they just stack up and rot."

"Sorry to interrupt, Madam President," said the Chief of Staff, "but your broadcast starts in three minutes, and everything is connected and working."

"Thanks, Donald." The President rose from her seat.

She glanced at the tablet in her hand and saw the notes that her aids had transmitted to her as suggested talking points. She considered saying something, as the pain in her chest had reached a new level and shot down her arm, too. She needed to get through this broadcast, and then she'd get it checked out. She could no longer ignore this.

President Russell approached the podium with the presidential seal digitally imprinted on the front screen. The technician started counting down from five, and she saw the green light appear on the camera.

"My fellow Americans—" Abby Russell said, and then she died from a massive occlusion of her left descending coronary artery. Her head bounced off the top of the podium as she collapsed. The hollow noise of her head striking the wood surface was the final sound that millions of people watching live, heard from the last person to serve as President of the United States.

Part Three

Chapter Thirty-One

YEAR 2023

THE NEARLY FULL JETLINER LANDED AT BOSTON'S LOGAN International Airport. Four hours earlier, it had departed from Brussels, Belgium. Onboard sat a young Army officer assigned to U.S. European Command as a junior information officer.

Sawyer Gomez had joined the U.S. Army after graduating from college, and had attended Officer Candidate School (OCS). Following the grueling twelve-week program, he'd become a commissioned officer with the rank of Second Lieutenant and was sent to Europe for his first assignment. Today was his first trip home in eighteen months. He'd come to enjoy military life and the opportunities it presented, but he missed his friends and family. Most of all, he missed his best friend, Devin Baker.

He looked forward to some time with Devin, especially considering everything that had been going on. Devin had become an international celebrity, and Sawyer knew that even in Europe people often spoke of the *healing man*.

The plane came to a stop, the *Fasten Seatbelt* light went off, and everyone got up and out of his or her seats. Sawyer grabbed his carryon bag and started toward the door, which opened to allow passengers to exit after a several minute wait.

He walked with the two hundred other passengers, into the customs area, where they had to turn over their immigration forms and present their passports to the officials from U.S. Customs and Border Protection for inspection. While standing in line, Sawyer repeatedly rubbed the right side of his neck. He'd slept most of the flight, and upon waking had a sore neck.

After a twenty-minute delay, he made it through the lines and was at the luggage carousel, where his large backpack waited for him. He grabbed it, slung it over his shoulder, and headed out the door which had a sign above it that read, *Ground Transportation*. Within five minutes, a shuttle bus stopped and picked him up and took him to the Blue Line T-station. The T was the public transportation for the city and surrounding area. This included commuter rail trains, buses, and subway trains.

Having grown up an hour and a half north of the city, Sawyer came into Boston regularly and knew his way around the subway system. He descended the stairs into the subway station and became aware of the smell that was present in all the subway stations in the system. It was a mix of the creosote from the rail ties, and heat and dust from the train brakes and the hot electric motors. Not unpleasant, just familiar. He smiled, realizing he was back home.

After a brief wait, the subway arrived, and he rode several stops to the Government Center Station. There, he changed to the Green Line to go a few more stops to the station for the Hynes Convention Center.

Once he exited the train, he walked to the escalator and took it up to street level. He turned and followed the signs for the brief walk to the convention center. As he did, he was again aware of the pain in his neck. As he approached the convention center, Sawyer was amazed to see the large sign for the convention center, and under it, in huge bright letters, *Devin Baker,* with two dates that were yesterday and today.

Sawyer followed a couple people toward the entrance. The woman looked to be in her mid-thirties and walked with an older teen who limped and was clearly in significant discomfort. Inside, there were several security guards and several staff members dressed in either suits or skirts. They were greeting everyone and giving them directions. The woman Sawyer had followed presented her smartphone, which displayed her e-ticket, and someone handed her a small clipboard and form.

"Please have this filled out and ready when your group is called back," said a man in a suit. "You're in group J, and Devin is currently with group F. It will be about ninety minutes until your group is called. I'll take you to the Group J waiting area. There are concessions available."

As they were led away to their waiting area, a well-dressed woman approached Sawyer.

"May I see your ticket, sir?"

He handed her his phone, with the digital pass that Devin had sent him. She took it, seemed confused for a second, and then realized what she was looking at.

"Oh! Are you Lieutenant Gomez?"

He smiled. "Yes, but please just call me Sawyer."

The woman took a radio from her pocket and spoke, "One-Eight, this is Candice. Our other VIP is here. I'll be bringing him back."

"Understood," came the reply, from the two-way radio.

"Sir, if you follow me, I'll take you back to the VIP area."

"I heard the other gentleman mention that there are concessions. Could we stop there? I haven't had anything to eat since leaving Belgium this morning, and I'm quite hungry."

The woman giggled. "You don't want the concession food. There's much better food waiting for you in the VIP reception area. I've known Devin for a few years now, and he speaks of you often."

"We grew up together. He's my best friend."

"He told me that you were the first person he told about his gift."

"That was a long time ago now. Probably about eight years. We were just teens when he discovered it. We did some experiments to see what all he could do. Back then, we had to keep everything secret. Neither of us would have imagined giant signs with his name on the front of a convention center.

"It's been quite a ride. I helped organize his first public healing event. He was very concerned when it came time to reveal his big secret," Candice explained.

She led him down a hall and made a few turns, then went through a door. It opened into a sizeable, fancy viewing platform, slightly above the main stage. Attendants in white tuxedos were serving food and beverages to the eight other people who had somehow earned VIP treatment.

A casually dressed man waited to greet them. "Sawyer!"

Sawyer froze for a second before he recognized the face of his childhood friend Tony Jiffers.

"Tony! What're you doing here?" Sawyer asked as he stepped forward and embraced his old friend.

"You didn't know? Candice and I are Devin's event coordinators. We set up all these trips and go with him to make sure everything runs smooth. Come look." Tony gestured for Sawyer to follow him over to the rail so they could look down to the stage. "Candice was one of the first people Devin healed. That was back when he was still experimenting. She has been coordinating these trips since the beginning. I came on a year ago to take some of the load off her."

Sawyer noticed the giant gold letters above the stage—DEVIN—and his mouth to dropped open. It wasn't anything like the subtlety that Devin had insisted on when they'd first started working with his abilities. Sawyer's initial impression was that this looked like something out of Las Vegas.

Down on the floor in front of the stage, he saw Devin seated in a high-back chair and people walking up to him. As they came up, Devin would glance at the clipboard and then touch them and watch the expression on their faces. Even from where Sawyer and Tony stood, they could see the reaction the people were having as their infirmities were cured.

Security guards were stationed on the floor, keeping the people in orderly lines. Some of the people that had come to see Devin were walking, while others were in wheelchairs, and a few on ambulance stretchers. All were waiting for their minute with the Healing Man.

"He really just sits there as they all parade by?" Sawyer said.

Tony chuckled. "No, he hates sitting and is usually walking the crowd. But after five to six hundred heals, he starts to get tired has to sit and rest from time to time. We did a huge show in LA a year ago, and by the end he couldn't lift his hand to put it on someone without one of us helping him. Since then, we limit the size of the events and often split them over two days."

"How many of these does he do?"

"We try to do one or two locations a week. Sometimes we do more if we're in a specific area. Last year, we started in Germany and did eight days in a row in different European cities. It was tiring for all of us, especially Devin. We did something similar a few months ago in East Asia. That time, we did six locations in ten days. That was much more relaxing, and we were able to have some fun, too."

"Wow! That's a huge amount of travel." Sawyer commented.

"True. But Devin purchased a Gulfstream G550, so we travel in comfort and don't have to deal with all the hassle of commercial flight. He wanted to get the newer G650, but there's a two-year wait."

"Sounds like a great way to travel. So exactly how does this all work? How do people get selected?

"We advertise three months ahead of time. They fill out

an application and send it in with a check or credit card number, for a thousand dollars. They have to list their infirmity and what relief they're hoping to get. If someone wants to grow back their amputated leg, we reject the application and refund the money. The desired outcome has to be something that's achievable. If the check bounces or the credit card payment doesn't clear, we shred the application and they're not considered.

Each applicant is allowed to come in with one additional person, usually a caregiver, spouse, or parent. They do a brief before-and-after video, where they describe their symptoms pre and post and we document any visible injury before and after. That way, if there's someone who wants their money back, we have video evidence that we helped them. Our target is eleven hundred people healed per event day. That way, after expenses, we clear about $1 million each day."

"Sounds like he's raking in the money."

"True. But we try to do charitable work, too. We try to visit one or more rehabilitation facilities or hospitals in each city. That's proving to be more difficult than you'd imagine. These facilities make their money off the patients, and if we swoop in and cure a bunch of them, that's lost revenue. They often don't want us there."

Sawyer and Tony heard something change down on the show floor, and they walked to the rail and saw the last of the group leaving the auditorium. Devin stood and looked up and to see his best friend for the first time in over two years. His huge smile was visible all the way up on the viewing platform. He said something to the security guard and jogged for the stairs.

Tony's radio beeped, and a voice said, "Devin will be taking a ten-minute break, and then we'll start with group G."

Devin entered from the far door and hurried to Sawyer, who met him halfway. They embraced the same way they always did, and the pain in Sawyer's neck vanished.

Devin took a step back after feeling something leave him and then return.

"What was wrong?"

Sawyer smiled. "Just a stiff neck from sleeping on the plane. But thanks." He moved his head side to side, feeling no discomfort.

"I'm so glad you came. It's great to see you!"

"I'm just glad I could come. You've got an amazing thing going here. You sure have come a long way from the days of us having to keep it all a secret."

"True. Everyone knows now. Hey, sorry to rush, but I need to get back on stage and I'm starving. Let's eat."

Devin led them over to a food bar that had covered food warmers and a salad bar. Looking at the selection, Sawyer was impressed to see grilled steak and shrimp, baked potatoes, and rice. There was also some pasta with Italian sausage in it.

Seeing his friend's reaction, Devin said, "I always make sure that my team is well-fed. There are usually twelve of us that go onsite, and I insist they're treated well."

"Well, this is very nice." Sawyer scooped some rice onto his plate, next to the steak and shrimp.

The friends sat, and Devin ate a few bites.

"Take your time and enjoy it," he said. "I need to get back on stage. I'll be done in about an hour and a half, and then we can take a walk and talk for a while. There's a nice coffee bar down the street."

"That works for me."

Devin hurried to eat his food and then raced back to work.

Sawyer walked to the rail to watch as the next group came in, led by Candice.

Chapter Thirty-Two

SAWYER WATCHED AS THE LAST GROUP EXITED THE auditorium. It had been interesting to observe as Devin had touched hundreds of people and their infirmities disappeared. From where he sat, Sawyer couldn't see everything, but he did see terrible scars disappear, limps and deformities vanish, and people who came in sitting in a wheelchair, pushing the empty chair away as they left. He also saw Devin get many hugs and more than a few kisses as well.

There was one thing that was noticeably absent. At no time did Devin or any of the staff hand out any kind of pamphlet explaining that this healing ability was a gift from God.

"Excuse me, Mr. Gomez," a security guard said.

"Yes?"

"They asked me to lead you down to the lower level. There's a little known back exit that Mr. Baker will use to leave, allowing him to avoid the crowds that are gathered out front, hoping to see him."

"Sounds good. Let's go." Sawyer shouldered his backpack and followed the guard down several halls and a flight of stairs.

At the bottom of the stairs, Devin was waiting. They thanked the security guard and headed out the door. Devin wore a ball cap, sunglasses, and a thick jacket that together helped hide his face and build.

"This usually does the trick," he said. "Sometimes people still recognize me. I make sure to not wander off by myself too often."

"A celebrity's life," Sawyer replied.

"True. It has its ups and downs. More ups than downs, fortunately. We can hit the coffee bar, and then there's a park next door where we can catch up for a while. At 5:00 p.m., we'll be picked up and taken to the airport for the short flight home. I made sure to save you a seat."

"Sounds great. Tony made the plane sound impressive."

"It is. I'm still sometimes confused about how I ended up here. Private planes and interviews. It all seems unreal."

"Don't forget, lots of hugs."

Devin snickered, shaking his head. "Sometimes too many. Usually it's nice, but a few of these people... they may be healed of their infirmities, but that doesn't mean their hygiene problems are fixed."

Both men laughed as they continued walking.

They entered the small but clean coffee shop and placed their orders. The woman behind the counter looked at Devin with a curious expression, but didn't say anything. Once the guys had their drinks, they headed out and across the street to a small park.

As they walked, Devin said, "You've heard all about my adventure. How's Belgium?"

"It's great! Brussels is a nice city, and the people are friendly. I've been learning the language, but almost everyone speaks passable English."

"What language do they speak there? German?"

Sawyer shook his head. "No, the official language is Dutch."

Devin nodded. "We've visited many European countries, but not Belgium yet. How is it being in the Army? Is it what you hoped?"

"I really enjoy it. I have lots of opportunities, and the work is mostly interesting. I'm seriously considering staying in after my first four years are up. Make a career of it."

"That's too bad. I'd hoped you'd work with us. We're getting to travel and see more of the world than you will even in the Army."

"I'll think about it. It is an interesting idea."

The friends entered the park and walked to a long row of connected picnic tables. Devin sat on one side, Sawyer the other, and they continued to discuss the Army for a while and then Sawyer changed the topic, "I need to ask something, and I don't want to offend you."

"Since when has that been a concern?" Devin smiled. "What is it?"

"Whatever happened to using your ability as a ministry? We designed the pamphlet for you to hand out. I didn't see anything like that today."

Devin's posture slumped and sadness entered his voice. "That was the plan. I even had a new brochure designed. It was very nice. Heck, we still have boxes of them in the office. Things just got moving so fast. I use to tell everyone how my ability was from God. Then we started moving eleven hundred people through at a time, and soon I realized that I'd stopped saying it. I had someone dedicated to handing out the brochures, but the events got so busy that she was always getting called upon to do other things. After a while, we weren't even taking the brochures with us because they took up space, they were heavy, and no one ever had time to distribute them."

The boys sat in silence for a few minutes, and then Devin got a text.

He looked at his phone and said, "The car will be here in

ten minutes to take us to the airport. You done with your cup?"

"Thanks." Sawyer handed over his empty cup.

Devin was walking toward the trash can, when a neon blue light appeared just in front of him.

"What's that!" Sawyer said.

Devin turned his head back toward Sawyer, while still walking. He'd hadn't seen the strange light. It started about three feet off the ground and grew to about six-feet high and three-feet wide.

Devin walked directly into it and disappeared.

Part Four

Chapter Thirty-Three

YEAR 2108

"What's that?" Devin heard his friend say.

He turned to look, not sure what Sawyer was talking about. Sawyer was seated at the table, looking at Devin... or maybe in front of him. Suddenly there was a brief feeling of warmth, and then everything changed. The park was gone. He was indoors, and the lighting was brighter than the overcast sky had been. Strange people were looking at him, and two were approaching and wore concerned looks. One was African-American, the other Caucasian. Both wore lab coats. As all this was registering, Devin almost collapsed. He was extremely week and sick to his stomach. His entire body hurt.

The two men grabbed his arms and guided him to a chair that a third person pushed close to him. As he sat, devices were attached to his forehead and chest.

"It's okay, Devin," said one of the two men.

In his confusion, Devin wasn't sure which.

"Sit here, and we will explain what's going on. But first, concentrate on healing yourself. That's why you're here."

"Maybe we should give him a dose. He isn't looking very good," said someone in the group.

"Yeah, we don't want to lose him, too," another voice said.

"Not yet. I don't want to interfere with his healing ability." The dark skinned man held a digital screen in his hands and kept switching his gaze from Devin to the screen. "Give him time to regenerate."

"Devin, I'm Doctor Matthew Becker, and this is Doctor Brian Stoffer," said the Caucasian man. "We aren't going to hurt you, and we will explain everything. We just need you to regenerate first, and then we can talk."

"What did you do to me?" Devin said, in a weak voice.

"I know this will sound crazy, but we're in the year 2108. We brought you eighty-five years into the future.'"

Brian Stoffer said, "The time travel process is extremely destructive to the body, which is why you feel so awful. Once your regenerative abilities kick in, you should feel much better. You will be the first person to jump through time and survive."

Devin felt a familiar sensation and became aware of the pain departing and the weakness decreasing. It seemed to take much longer than ever before for the healing process to complete. Instead of a few seconds, the sensation of his body healing seemed to take a few minutes. Eventually, the process ended and Devin, though tired, felt normal. The people who had been keeping him from toppling out of the chair, stepped back as he pushed himself to his feet.

"Devin, how are you feeling? Brian said.

"Back to normal, I think." Devin answered as he took an offered glass of water. "Where am I?"

"We're in a private laboratory," Matthew said, "located in what's now known as Mid-Atlantic Region, Military District Six. You would know it as Virginia, just outside Alexandria."

"Military District Six? What does that mean? Why did you bring me here?"

"I'm sorry for all this, Devin," replied Matthew, "but it's a very long story, and some of it will probably be upsetting to you."

"Are you able to send me home?"

"Certainly. Right now I could send you back as easily as I brought you here. Why don't you follow us? We're going to move to a conference room which will be more comfortable."

Brian set the digital screen on a table and told the group, "Everything looks normal now, but I caught some interesting data before and during his regeneration."

Devin looked around the room. It was a large room full of high-tech equipment. There was a large glowing arch in the center of the room and workstations with strange-looking equipment installed on them. There was also a wheeled stretcher with a balled-up stained sheet pushed against the wall. On the table next to him sat a plastic container. In it lay a belt, two small plastic bottles, a crumpled piece of paper, and a couple small devices that Devin didn't recognize. There was also a hospital ID badge with a woman's face and the name *Abby Russell* on it. He recognized the ID badge. It was from the same hospital where he was born and had later conducted some of the tests of his capabilities.

The three of them got up and walked out of the lab and down the hall. As they passed some floor to ceiling windows, Devin slowed to look outside. It was a cloudy day, and there was a light rain falling. There were strange-looking military vehicles and troops stationed up and down the block. A helicopter gunship seemed to be circling the area.

"What's going on? Are we under some kind of attack?"

"No, Devin," said Brian. "This place is probably the safest location in the country. No one can get within a half-mile of this location. The military has it completely locked down."

"Why?"

"Because of you," Matthew said. "You see, we created you."

Chapter Thirty-Four

DEVIN STOPPED WALKING. "WHAT DO YOU MEAN YOU CREATED me?"

"Step in here and have a seat." Brian held the conference room door open. "We will explain everything." He looked at Matthew. "Start telling him what happened. I need to make the call."

Devin and Matthew entered the room. Devin looked around at the plain-looking room. There was nothing on the walls, and other than the large table and matching chairs, there was nothing else. It felt cold and impersonal.

They sat, and Matthew said, "We will tell you everything. We have no reason to hold anything back. However, some of what I tell you might be a bit difficult, okay?"

Devin nodded.

"As we said, we brought you eighty-five years into the future. For the first eighty-three of those eighty-five years, things progressed as you might expect. There were technological advancements, political changes, and a few small or regional wars. The United States increased to fifty-two states, but basically was the same. Then two years ago, a lab in

Arizona was illegally researching the weaponization of man-made viruses for military use. An incident occurred, and the most contagious pathogen imaginable was released into the world."

Brian paused and saw Devin nod indicating that he followed what was being explained.

"The pathogen wiped out close to 80 percent of the world's population. Many governments collapsed, and one-third of the nations that existed before, no longer do. Either they're in a state of anarchy, or a new nation is rising from what's left. Here in the U.S., most of the government leaders have died from the disease. The President and Vice President are dead. Most of those in the line of succession were gone, and many that survived were in hiding, not wanting to get the illness. The military took over and worked aggressively to restore order. It has been two years, and there are large areas of the country that are still ungoverned, with no one really in charge. Of the parts that are in military control, only 70 percent have electricity. There just aren't enough people to maintain order and restore services."

As Matthew finished the history, Brian returned catching the end of the explanation

"So you want to send me back in time to cure people of the disease?" Devin asked.

"No, not all," Matthew replied.

The answer surprised Devin as this seemed to be the logical explanation.

"At the time when this disaster struck," Brian said, "I had been working in medical research, looking for ways to make the human body heal much faster. My problem was that from the time my serum was administered, it looked like it could be decades before the ability to regenerate faster manifested." He looked at Matthew and nodded.

"And I was working on a process for moving objects back

and forth in time," Matthew said. "My time travel system worked, but was destructive to biomatter—plant and animal cells, that is. We worked together and improved both processes. The time travel is still fatal to anyone that uses it. Unless, of course, they have the ability to heal at the cellular level and at an enhanced rate. You weren't created to be able to heal anyone, but simply to be able to survive time travel. The truth is that we never thought you'd be able to heal others. That's an unplanned side effect, which we can't explain. You see, just last week we got to the point where we decided that we were ready to attempt this on human subjects. Over the last few days, we've sent a total of six volunteers, one at a time, on what were basically suicide missions. They received heavy doses of IV medications to strengthen their cells, and they went back in time. Each had a dose of the serum to allow for rapid healing with them. Their instructions were to inject a specific subject while still an infant. Hopefully as those babies grew up, they would develop the ability to regenerate rapidly and would be available for our purposes. Our volunteers going back in time knew they would only have, at most, thirty minutes to accomplish their mission before their bodies failed. Of the six, two never returned, and it doesn't seem they were successful in injecting their infants. They may well not have survived long enough to get their mission completed. Number three completed their mission and returned, but the advanced healing ability never seemed to develop as the subject got older. Number four developed self-healing abilities, which we discovered by looking back on their decades' old medical records. There were notes, and even news articles, about a miraculous self-healing ability. Unfortunately, when she was pulled eighty-five years into the future, she died before being able to start regenerating. The fifth subject received a double dose of the serum, as did you, but she died in a freak drowning accident as a teen before her ability manifested."

"Is that making sense so far?" Brian said.

"I guess so," Devin replied.

"That brings us to you," Matthew said. "Number six. This morning, a brave woman, knowing she would not survive, traveled back to the day of your birth. She injected you with a double dose of the serum my team and I created. Two hours ago, she returned dead. We then began searching for you online and discovered that there had been a Devin Baker who lived decades ago and had an amazing ability. Able to heal others and himself. We looked for a time when our historical records indicated that your ability seemed to have peaked, and then snatched you up from that time period and brought you here."

"All this time I thought that my healing ability was a gift from God."

"Sorry to tell you this, Devin, but your healing ability is the result of two imperfect scientific experiments pulled together out of desperation."

Devin processed the incredible information he'd received.

After a few minutes, he said, "Why me? Why did you pick me from all the other people in the past to use? I know I was number six, but what got me on the list?"

"It was random. We had the computer look for someone that was deceased but had lived a full life. Not too far in the past—there had to be computer records available. Also, there had to be nothing significant about their lives. We couldn't pull someone to the future who was supposed to make a significant contribution to society."

Devin though for a minute. "So that means, if I hadn't been changed to have this healing ability, I would have been a nobody? Contributing nothing to society?"

The two scientists looked at one another.

"I wouldn't put it like that," Matthew said. "You lived a decent life, but nothing that was noteworthy in the big picture."

Devin slumped his shoulders and looked down at the floor. Apparently without the healing ability, his overall life would have meant very little to society. Eventually, he said, "OK, so what do you want from me?"

"When the disaster unfolded," Matthew said, "my company worked with the civilian government, and later the military government, to produce the vaccine against the disease as quickly as possible. This got me the opportunity to speak to the upper leadership of the country. The official U.S. government collapsed when the President died, and there was no one willing or able to take over. We were all fortunate that it was General Marcus Quimby, the former Chairman of the Joint Chiefs, who seized power. He provided solid leadership at a time when we had none. There are some people who would call some of his acts brutal, but he quickly ended the civil unrest and brought order out of chaos. Fortunately, the man is a Red, White and Blue patriot and is determined to restore the civilian government. He has no desire to rule any longer than needed. I met with him to discuss the production of the vaccine, and also told him about the work that Brian and I are doing. He's eager to see this project completed, and he provides us security and the needed resources. Our goal is to go back in time and prevent the disaster from ever happening. But to do that, we need someone who can survive time travel."

Devin looked at them and thought about all he'd heard. It was overwhelming.

After a minute, he said, "Is it even possible to change the past? I once read something that said going back in time can't change the present."

"Over the decades, there have been many theories, lots of ideas about what can be done with time travel. Current thinking among most quantum theorists is that time is linear, and changes in the past directly influence the future. Some of our basic testing would support that thought process. Therefore, what you go back and do will be able to prevent the disaster."

"So my mission is to go back in time and save the world?" Devin asked suspiciously.

"No. You need to go back in time and pass a message to someone."

Chapter Thirty-Five

General Marcus Quimby sat in the cramped rear compartment of the military transport helicopter. The general, a tall, powerfully built man, was in his early sixties, with graying hair. He was studying data on a thin tablet computer which was about twice the size of the standard pocket comp. The general's aide sat next to him, anticipating what information would be requested next.

The ultra-fast aircraft made its way toward the secure airspace surrounding the industrial complex owned by Stoffer Medical Enterprise. Since the global pandemic, this facility had become one of the most heavily guarded places in the U.S.

An hour ago, Brian Stoffer had contacted the general directly—something he'd never done before. He was excited to explain that there had been a massive break in their efforts, and encouraged the general to come to their facility as soon as possible. The general had been attending a briefing at Mid-Atlantic Regional Military Headquarters. They were discussing the next-quarter goals for returning power and essential services to several regions. Many areas were still impacted by lack of manpower, making it nearly impossible to keep things running.

The U.S. offered ration cards to anyone wishing to immigrate. Workers were desperately needed, and everyone over fifteen years old was required to work full-time. There were no exceptions, and the consequences for providing food to anyone who didn't have a current employment card were harsh. The problem is that most other nations also offered similar benefits, and transportation between nations was almost nonexistent. Instability was prevalent in many countries, and the extreme international anger toward the U.S. for its part in the pandemic was still present.

Most Americans agreed that if it weren't for the bold moves of Marcus Quimby to seize power and restore order, the nation would have collapsed. Marcus hoped that the history books would agree with that. However, there were some, who weren't pleased with the strict requirements placed on all citizens and the current military rule. The general agreed with this and was anxious for the return to civilian rule and the election of a President, which had been delayed due to the need to restore essential services. Right now, the military's strength advanced this needed work a lot faster than if they weren't in control.

His personal goal was for there to be general elections within the next year. An even better solution would be if Brian Stoffer and his team were able to complete this time travel project. Then the entire disaster could be prevented.

General Quimby felt the aircraft bank to the left and became aware of the airspeed rapidly decreasing. They were getting ready to land. He handed the tablet back to his aide, who returned it to a small backpack he was responsible for. A second aide carried another pack that was always close to the general. Years ago, it was referred to as the nuclear football. No longer thought of in that way, it still contained the nuclear launch codes and was all the general needed to launch a nuclear attack on any target in the world.

With all the upheaval and anger in the world at the time he took control of the U.S. government, the general would often lay awake at night, terrified that he might have to use that option. Fortunately, the sixteen nuclear powers considered the loss of additional lives to be such a high risk that no one had crossed that line.

The aircraft came to a mid-air stop and descended until Marcus Quimby felt the wheels touch the ground. After receiving the all-clear from the pilot, the general's aide opened the door and let the commanding general exit the aircraft. He was met by his Secret Service detail, which had arrived just before him in a similar aircraft. Unlike the Secret Service of the nation's previous leaders, these men and women wore full combat gear and carried a variety of weapons.

General Quimby noticed Matthew Becker patiently waiting just outside the barriers surrounding the helicopter landing pad and headed to meet the scientist.

"Good afternoon, General."

"Matthew, good to see you again. Where's Brian?"

"General, we did it! We brought our subject here from eighty-five years in the past, and he survived. Brian is with him now."

"You actually did it? It really worked?" The general responded, the amazement evident in his voice. He had desperately wanted their plan to work, but never actually thought it would.

"It did. Come, you can see." Matthew turned and led the general inside.

"Matthew, my people here informed me that there are five dead bodies from your experiments this morning, and that your team asked for them to be gotten rid of."

"Unfortunately, that's true. All but one of the deceased were volunteers who knew what would happen."

The general nodded. "You guys warned me this could happen. Should we be expecting more?"

"Probably not. Now that we brought someone here that can survive the process, we're almost at the finish line. Hopefully this guy, Devin, will complete the mission."

As Matthew explained, the door leading into the facility slid open, triggered by his biochip.

"Amazing! So when will this Devin be ready for this mission?"

"Not sure. We started briefing him after we called you. We have to make sure he's fully in agreement and knows what he has to do. Brian was just finishing a complete medical examination on him when I came to get you. He may need to rest a day. He survived the time jump, but it was very hard on him physically. We need to know that he's fully regenerated before we send him through again."

As they approached the elevator, the doors opened and two Secret Service agents were already inside. The elevator car and downstairs lab area were already confirmed as secure by the agents.

The group exited the elevator and headed down the corridor to the conference room, where Doctor Brian Stoffer and Devin sat chatting, and a female agent stood at attention next to them.

General Quimby looked at his security detail. "We're going to need some privacy, please."

The lead agent nodded and directed the others to take positions on the outside of each of the conference room's two doors.

Chapter Thirty-Six

WHEN THE NEW ARRIVALS ENTERED THE ROOM, BRIAN STOOD. "Hello, General. We're glad you could make it here. This is Devin Baker. Devin, this is General Marcus Quimby. He's the current Commander in Chief of what's left of our nation."

Devin stood and was confused about what to say or do. He'd never spoken to someone holding military rank before.

He stuck out his hand. "Good to meet you, sir."

The general took the offered hand. "I'm glad to meet you, Devin. From what I'm hearing, you might be the most important person in the whole world right now."

"That is what they're telling me, and that makes me very uncomfortable."

"Devin, do you understand how bad our situation is? How bad the pandemic has damaged the human race?" The general asked.

"I think so. It sounds like about 80 percent of the population was wiped out almost overnight. They told me that the rebuilding is extremely slow because there are no people to do the work."

"Very true, Devin. We're encouraging women to reproduce at high rates. We want families to have ten kids each. But that won't help until the children are older. So for the first fifteen years, we're making the situation worse. We will have a surge in the need for daycare workers and teachers. Also, many of these pregnant women will be out of the workforce for a significant amount of time. We can't afford that. We need lots more people, but don't have the resources to provide for them. The disaster didn't end when the disease was wiped out. It still continues now, several years later."

"So the easy answer is to have someone prevent it from ever happening," Brian said. "However, until now, something like that has never been possible."

"But we have that ability," said Matthew. "The technology works. We also have the only person who's able to survive the time travel process."

"So when I go back, exactly what am I expected to do?"

"Well, Devin," the general said, "it's not hard, or even dangerous. I'll give you a pocket comp, which you'll deliver to me in the past, at an address that I provide."

"What's a pocket comp?"

The general gave Devin a confused look and then glanced at the other two men.

Brian smiled. "Remember, General, we just pulled him from eighty-five years in the past. He's never heard of one."

Quimby nodded. "A pocket comp is just what it sounds like. It's a pocket-sized computer that interacts with your biochip. Do you know what a biochip is?"

Devin shook his head, starting to feel overwhelmed. "No, I've never heard of that either."

"Don't worry," Brian said. "We'll take care of that before you go back. Nevertheless, a biochip is a type of nanochip injected under the skin on your arm. It allows you to interact online. Anything from financial transactions to opening locked doors. Among other things, it replaced bank cards and paper currency. It also serves as your identification. In our time, it would be impossible to do much of anything without it."

"So you'll deliver a pocket comp to me," Quimby said. "It might be difficult to get past my security, so I'll give you several pieces of information to help with that. Once I have all the information from the comp, I'll prevent this from ever happening."

As the meeting progressed, food was delivered and they relaxed, discussing plans and timing. The conversation had been pleasant, and Devin had found General Quimby to be quite personable.

Unfortunately, Devin's abilities didn't reduce his need for sleep. Since he'd spent most of the day at the convention center, healing over a thousand people, he was exhausted. The stress on him from having to heal himself after the jump through time just made the fatigue worse. It wasn't long before he needed to excuse himself from the conversation. But first, one nagging question remained.

"I need to ask something. I understand the situation and why I have to do this. Now, when I first got to this time, you said you were able to send me home. How will I get back home after I save the world for you? From the year you're sending me to, three years ago, your time travel technology won't exist for several years. Also, it seems like your time travel only works now because you had the pandemic to push your work faster."

The room got quiet, and the three men from this time period looked at one another.

"We did tell you that we could send you back," Brian said. "We can do that right now. However, if you go back in time three years and stop this disaster, we won't really have a way to get you back home after that. This current time, where the ability to move you through time exists, won't ever exist. We were able to bring back the volunteers we sent out because they didn't change the situation that brought our time travel technology into existence. When you prevent the pandemic, you will erase everything that brought our technology to where it is today. I know that's confusing, and not what you wanted to hear."

"I think that makes sense. And that is what I thought the answer would be. I will be stuck at a time three years ago," Devin stated with dejection in his voice. After a moment to think, he said, "Let me see one of those pocket comps. Show me how to use it."

Matthew picked his up from the table, powered it on and slid it to Devin. "What is it you want to do?"

"I want to do a search on myself and see what happened after I disappeared."

"After we had you injected with my serum," Brian said, "we looked that up. You continued to do your healing events for many years. But for the last twenty years of your life, you retreated to a remote villa in France and lived out your last days in relative seclusion, only occasionally making an appearance when someone prominent was sick or injured. You're able to heal from injury and disease, but the normal aging process isn't stopped for you."

Matthew shook his head. "That's not what he means. That was what happened because we injected him and gave him the healing ability. But that all changed when we brought him here. That version of history no longer exists."

Devin nodded and found that these multiple versions of history made sense to him, in a strange way.

"Exactly." He took the pocket comp and started inputting his request.

The interface was close enough to a web browser from his time that he quickly figured out how to use it. The performance was impressive. There was none of the lag he would have experienced on his old smartphone.

Devin switched from one news article to another. The first headline from eighty-five years in the past read, *The Healing Man Disappears*, followed by another that said, *The Mysterious Disappearance of Devin Baker*. There were several others with similar titles. He skimmed through them. Then another title caught his eye—*An Arrest Has Been Made in the Devin Baker Case.* He selected the article.

U.S. Army Second Lieutenant Sawyer Gomez has been detained and is being questioned in the disappearance of the famous healer, Devin Baker. Gomez admittedly was the last person with Devin Baker before he disappeared. The initial questioning of Lieutenant Gomez produced answers that authorities say don't make sense, and he is now considered a suspect in the Healing Man's disappearance.

Devin felt his hands getting clammy and his anxiety building as he read the next headline. *Charges Filed in the Disappearance of Devin Baker.* This article was linked to another that was dated almost a year later. *Gomez acquitted in the disappearance of Devin Baker.* Devin read it and saw a statement from the jury foreman, which said, *"The prosecution failed to show proof that Lieutenant Gomez did anything criminal, even though his description of the events still seems impossible."*

Devin scrolled up one last time and saw another headline. *Army to Discharge Sawyer Gomez Following his Trial in the Devin Baker Case.* He set the pocket comp on the table and slid it back to Matthew.

General Quimby saw the look of despair on his face. "What did you learn?"

For a long moment, Devin said nothing and then broke his silence "Sawyer is my best friend. He has been since we were little kids. He was with me when you brought me here. There was no one else around. They arrested him. They think he did something to me. There was even a trial."

There was complete silence in the room.

"I am not going to help you. You need to send me back."

"Devin, I really am sorry about what happened to your friend Sawyer," the general said. "I truly am. But what we need you to do is much, much bigger than your friend."

Devin snapped, feeling anger boil up as he rarely had before, "Sawyer is my best friend! He is an officer in the U.S.

Army, just like you." He stabbed his finger at Quimby. "I won't do this to him!"

The three men sat in silence and avoided looking at Devin. Each was trying to think of something to say, but came up empty.

After minutes of uncomfortable silence, Devin stood and left the room.

Chapter Thirty-Seven

DEVIN ROLLED OVER, SLOWLY WAKING UP. AN IV LINE WAS still secure in his arm. He had reluctantly allowed Brian Stoffer to start an infusion of a medication that supposedly strengthened the cells so that they better withstood the effects of time travel. This was the same compound he'd given the volunteers who had traveled back in time to create Devin. Since he had been subjected to a time jump once and no one was sure how another move through time so soon would affect him, they weren't taking any chances.

He had only agreed to the IV when Brian and Matthew promised to find a way to accomplish the mission and still get him back to his time. They also pointed out that this would be necessary even if they just sent him home.

Devin took the blanket off and swung his legs over the side of the makeshift cot. They'd converted a small lab area into a room where he could sleep. It was dark and quiet, and that was all he needed to fall asleep. He reached down to the floor, found his jeans and slid out his smartphone. It couldn't connect to the network here, which was far too advanced, but it could tell him how long he'd slept—nine hours. He looked at the IV bag and saw that it was had emptyied while he slept, so he freed the tubing from his arm and yanked the catheter out of his wrist. The tiny hole closed up before a single drop of blood came out. He finished dressing and walked out the door.

After stopping in a restroom, Devin headed down the hall. He found his way back to the conference room with help from a member of General Quimby's security detail. Matthew and the general were seated at the table, along with other members of Brian's and Matthew's project teams. A spread of food was available, and Devin headed for a seat.

"Good morning, Devin," said General Quimby.

"Morning, everyone." Devin nodded to the group.

"Did you sleep okay?" Matthew said. "Any side effects from the medications you received?"

"No. I was exhausted and slept great. Now I'm really hungry."

Matthew smiled. "While you slept, we came up with a solution to the problem of getting you back home. I will prepare a pocket comp. Once you've completed your mission, you'll use it. It has instructions on how to find me. I'll be able to contact Brian and explain it to him so he can help. It also contains all the information I'll need to advance the time travel technology so we can send you home."

Devin eye's grew wide. "I had assumed it wouldn't be possible, but I hadn't even considered that there could be an easy solution like this."

"Once you find me, using the data you have, we will be able to make the needed improvements to my processes. It might take a month or two, but I can do it."

"Devin, will that be acceptable?" Quimby said.

"I think so. I can't see why it wouldn't work."

Devin could see the relief on the faces of the men sitting around the table.

He then asked a question that had come to him as he was

waiting to get to sleep the night before, "Do you mind if I ask you guys something personal?"

"Sure," Matthew replied. "What do you want to know."

"You told me how devastating the disaster was. Did you guys lose anyone?"

The three men shared glances.

"My daughter survived," Matthew said. "My wife and son didn't."

"I recognized what was going on early," said Brian, "and immediately quarantined my wife and three kids in our home until the vaccine became available. We were very lucky."

There was a pause, before General Quimby said, "I had three grown kids. Two were married, and the other engaged. There were also five grandchildren. My daughter's fiancé survived. None of the rest made it. My wife had passed a few years before from cancer."

There was silence around the table. Devin thought about how much this man had lost, and then in just a few weeks he had the responsibility of the entire nation dropped on top of him. His current admiration for the general took a giant leap.

"I am very sorry for all that you lost, General," said Devin. "I will do everything I can to prevent it."

General Quimby nodded, and getting back on track said, "Go ahead and eat, and I'll tell you the plan we've been developing. I'll give you two identical pocket comps. They can only be unlocked with either my biochip or the one you'll have. You will go to my home address. My security will stop you, and you'll need to show them one of the videos on the comp. That should convince them to let you see me. After that, you just give me the comp and I'll do the rest."

"That doesn't sound too difficult. But what about this biochip?" Devin asked.

"Everyone gets a biochip at a young age," Matthew said. "As they get older, it's enabled to do more and more. Sensors in the doors read the chip to allow access to the right people.

In stores and restaurants, the sales systems query the chip and transfer funds electronically to cover purchases. All computers can access the biochip to allow proper access. These are just a few examples. It is illegal to tamper with or copy a biochip. Right now, my tech team is working on cloning my biochip. You'll get the clone. When you go back, everything will identify you as being me. You'll be able to request a car or make a purchase, as needed. The pocket comps you're carrying will work for you because you've got that chip in you."

"Why clone yours? Can't I just get my own?" Devin asked.

"That's what we were going to do until we realized that it wouldn't work. Any account we create for your biochip today won't exist several years ago. Your chip would be worthless. You need a biochip that had an account back then,"

"Won't you notice that there's someone else using your identity and report me?"

"The pocket comp that you're taking back to give me will explain it all to me. You should have time to complete your mission with the general and find me before I would notice any strange activity on my accounts."

Devin sat quietly, thinking about his situation.

"Devin, something's troubling you," Brian said. "We can see it on your face. What is it?"

"I doubt this will make sense to you. But for years, I thought I was supposed to use this gift to heal people. That it was a gift from God. I thought that was my purpose. Now I find that none of what I thought about who I am is real. It's hard to process."

"Devin, you say you wanted to use this gift to help people," General Quimby said. "Now you'll be saving the lives of over eight billion people. I understand what you're saying, but you have a different purpose—an alternate purpose."

Chapter Thirty-Eight

DEVIN ENTERED THE LAB, THE SAME PLACE WHERE HE HAD first appeared when they pulled him into the future. While walking, he unconsciously rubbed the spot on his right arm where the cloned biochip had been injected an hour before. There wasn't any pain or discomfort, just a sensation, and he knew there was now futuristic technology added to his body.

He stopped only a few feet into the room and looked in amazement at what he saw. He was taking more time to survey the room than when he was last here. There were multiple workstations around the room, with strange-looking equipment. What was most impressive was how few computer monitors there were. Instead, most of the displays were holographic. Text and imagery, including video, were displayed in the air around the stations. The clarity of the video images was as good as if there had been a screen.

Devin shifted his gaze to the center of the room, where there was a large arch. He had seen it briefly the day before, when he'd first arrived. It was about ten-feet high and two-feet thick. The arch was wide enough to drive a small car through, and glowed with a pulsating neon blue light. The blue light transfixed him, as it seemed to get brighter and brighter.

Devin jumped when he became aware that someone had come up behind him, to his left.

"Incredible, isn't it," Brian said.

"How does it work?"

"Matthew has tried to explain it to me, but I can't follow the physics. Somehow, time and space are manipulated, and a portal to another time is opened. If I hadn't seen it work, I wouldn't believe it. As it's storing energy and opening the portal, those blue pulsations get faster."

The two men continued to watch the pulsing lights for several seconds.

"So are you ready?" Brian said.

"I guess. My task is rather simple. My biggest concern is how long it will take you and Matthew to get me home when I'm done."

"That additional comp you're taking will allow us to fairly quickly advance our projects. Getting us from where they were two years ago to what we have now won't be too hard. We should be able to send you home in just a month, maybe a little more."

"I told everyone that my ability was a gift from God. Now I'll go back with a different story. I feel like a fraud. I don't know that I can go back to doing what I had been."

"You mean the big healing events you conduct? You make quite a bit of money from them."

"How do you know about them?"

"They're what made it so easy for us to know our experiment would work. We randomly picked you from a historic online profile. Researched you online and saw that there was nothing unusual about you. Exactly what we wanted. We sent our volunteer back to inject you with the serum just after you were born. A few minutes later, we did an Internet search on you again, and then there was lots of information about your healing ability. Many articles were written about your healing sessions and how profitable they were. There was no doubt from the old articles we read that our experiment hadn't just worked, but there was an unexpected side effect. You could heal others, too."

"I still can't believe that wasn't by design. Healing myself is great, but when I can help many others, this ability means so much more."

Matthew and General Quimby entered the room. Matthew carried a blue backpack.

The general approached Devin. "It's an amazing thing. Isn't it?"

"It sure is. This whole thing is amazing. Part of me doesn't want to believe it, and the rest knows it's true. I just want to get this problem handed off to you... well, to the you of the past."

"Devin, the system is almost ready," Matthew said. "This pack has everything you'll need. A primary and backup comp for the general, one for you to give to me after the mission is complete, and one for you for any information you might need. So there are four in all. There's also some packaged food and bottles of water, as well as a rain poncho and a change of clothes. I'm sorry that the food we're sending isn't appetizing, but we had to choose items that would survive the passage through time. There aren't many edible items that meet that criteria. If you need to make any purchases, you can do that through the biochip."

"Okay, that all sounds good. But there is one more question."

"What is it?" Matthew asked.

"If I go back and prevent the disaster by giving General Quimby the message. Then the pandemic never happens. Without the pandemic, there will be no reason for you to send volunteers back in time to give me the healing ability. Then I will never be able to survive time travel."

Matthew smiled, "That is called a temporal paradox. A change in time prevents something from happening that led to that change, so that change never happens. There are theories around such things, but since you're the first to travel in time, nothing is proven. The best I can tell you is that contemporary thinking is that since you're the one moving between two time-lines you are not impacted by a change that happen in the timeline. Basically, you will be carrying the ability with you as you cross to another time."

Devin thought for a minute and then said, "But that is just a theory. Right?"

"I am afraid that's the best we have. There have been no tests to prove it one way or another."

Devin's face fell as he realized that his getting home was not a certainty, "That isn't very encouraging, but I guess there's no choice now. What do I need to do next?"

"Follow me over here," Matthew said. "When the system is ready, you'll walk through the arch."

Devin moved to where he was instructed and watched the light in the arch pulsate faster and faster. Then a spot of light, the same color as the arch, formed and grew to the size of a door.

Chapter Thirty-Nine

YEAR 2105

MADISON PARK, LOCATED IN FALLS CHURCH, VIRGINIA, IS A 2.7-acre family-friendly park with lots of amenities. This evening, light rain was falling in the deserted park. Suddenly a spot of bright neon blue light appeared at about waist height. It grew in height and width, and within five seconds, it had grown to about the size of a door. Devin stepped through the portal, then it faded and disappeared.

He stumbled and looked for something to hold onto and a place to sit. As planned, he was next to a pavilion with several picnic tables under it. He grabbed hold of the closest of the shelter's wood legs to keep his balance as he worked his way to one of the covered picnic tables and dropped onto the seat.

He felt extremely weak and was having trouble concentrating. His entire body was painful, and he knew that he was suffering from massive cellular disruption. It felt like it took forever, but it was only about thirty seconds before he felt a familiar sensation throughout his body. The pain was gone and his strength returned. He remained seated for several minutes until all the symptoms fully subsided. While he could survive and quickly recover from the effects of time travel, it was the most miserable thing he'd ever experienced, and he would be glad to put it behind him when they got him home.

Slowly, he stood and followed the path through the park. Devin was only about a quarter-mile from General Quimby's residence. He walked at a fast pace, wanting to arrive before it got too late in the evening. After exiting the park, he turned left on North Street, and followed it past two large houses, and then turned left on Vintage Avenue. The general's house was the second one ahead, on the right. It was a two-story brick-faced building with a large staircase running from the sidewalk up to the door. As expected, Devin noticed the car sitting at the curb with the engine running. He removed the first pocket comp from the pack. It was a select model not ordinarily available to civilians. It was already powered on and he did a search for nearby biochips. It displayed the one for Matthew Becker, which was illegally in Devin's arm. There was also one nearby for Warren Black. Devin recognized the name from the briefing the general had given him, and pulled up a specific video.

With all the confidence he could conjure up, and reminding himself that no one could harm him, Devin boldly approached the passenger door, opened it and dropped into the seat as if he owned the vehicle.

He was briefly confused to see that there wasn't a steering wheel, until he remembered the conversation he'd had with Brian Stoffer about all the technological advancements in the last eighty-five years.

"What are you doing?" said Agent Warren Black. "Get out! This is an official government vehicle."

"Hello," Devin said, in the friendliest voice he could, "Your name is Warren Black. You're married to Cynthia Black, formerly Cynthia Stout. You have two sons, Kevin and Dakota. You're employed with the Federal Protection Service and are currently assigned to protect General Quimby. Your partner is in the house. Do I have your attention?"

"Who are you?"

"My name is Devin. I need you to look at this."

Devin pushed an icon on the screen of the pocket comp and played the recording that the general had made for Warren. There were seven other recordings, all ready for whoever from the Federal Protection Service happened to be on duty tonight.

Warren had no choice but to accept the device that Devin pushed into his hands. He looked at the screen and saw the face of General Quimby.

"Warren, I'm sorry that this is so unusual, but I need you to trust Devin and bring him to me, in the house. This is of critical importance, and we can't explain any more right now. I understand that this is strange and you have doubts. So to allow you to trust that this message is really from me, do you remember the conversation you and I had last summer at the picnic? When your son Dakota commented on how attractive my daughter is. He didn't know that I was her father, and I was standing at your side when he said it. You later said that was the most embarrassing moment in your life. We'll both laugh about that forever. Now please bring Devin to me. Feel free to scan him for weapons and explosives, but let him keep the blue bag he's carrying."

The recording ended, and Devin took the pocket comp from Warren's hand.

"I'm sorry, Agent Black, but I needed to get your attention and the general said this would do it."

Warren glanced at the backpack, noting that it was indeed blue.

After a few seconds to think about what he had heard, he said, "There's a lot more going on here than I realize, isn't there?"

Warren thought about the pocket comp he'd just held. He had recently upgraded his wife's to the newest model, one that had just come onto the market. and this one was a generation newer. It wasn't expected to be available for another two years, according to an article he'd recently read.

"Quite true," Devin answered as he opened the car door.

Warren got out of the car, took a device from the console, and approached Devin. He scanned him and the bag, and had a perplexed expression as he looked at the results.

"OK, let's go," he said.

The two of them approached the eight steps leading to the front door, and Warren reached for his collar and activated a hidden control.

"Two coming in," he said into the device.

When they got to the top step, Warren stopped and looked at Devin.

"The General Quimby in your video looks a little older than I'd expect."

"He's been through a lot," Devin answered with a slight smile.

Warren nodded, his suspicion confirmed. However, he had no idea what it meant. They met another agent as they entered the house.

"Bill, please go and get the general. Tell him there's a visitor and that we'll be in his study."

With a confused look, the junior agent nodded and left to summon General Quimby. Devin followed Warren to the study and they both stood, waiting by the door.

Three minutes later, Marcus Quimby approached, dressed casually in light pants, a t-shirt, and slippers.

"Sorry to bother you, sir," Warren said, "but this sounded like it might be urgent."

Quimby looked at Devin, clearly trying to determine how this young man could have something so urgent. He waved both of them into the study and shut the door.

Devin surveyed the room and was impressed with the expensive decor, wood-paneled walls, and the many military commendations on display.

Again, Devin took control before anyone else could. He

approached the general and guided him a few feet away from Agent Warren Black.

"General, my name is Devin Baker. Your Defense Department authorization code is 95832140Z."

The general paused with a blank look. "How could you possibly know that? I'm the only one who knows that code."

Devin pressed the pocket comp into the general's hands, another video ready to go.

"Sir, please sit and hit play."

The general, not used to being told what to do, scowled but still walked to his desk, pulled out the chair and sat.

"Sir, you might not want anyone else to hear this right now."

"Warren, I think we're all set."

"Yes, sir. I'll be right outside the door if you need me." He slipped out of the study and closed the door behind him.

Devin sat and remained silent. He didn't want to be a distraction while Marcus watched the video.

Marcus Quimby gave Devin one more disapproving look and pressed play. Devin smiled as General Quimby came face to face with his future self and paled.

It took a full fifteen minutes for him to watch the video. Several times he glanced up at Devin, who smiled and nodded each time.

When he finished, he looked up at Devin. "Are you hungry?"

"Yes sir, I am."

Quimby pushed a button on his desk. "Attendant, please send in some sandwiches. We're working late. There are two of us in here." To Devin he said, "Time travel? Really?"

Devin nodded.

"And you're from the future?"

"Actually, I'm just delivering a message from the future."

The general looked confused again, clearly not sure what Devin meant by that. "And I'm the President?"

"Yes, sir. But since you weren't elected, you refuse to use that title. And you hate it. Actually, you hate the fact that you had to grab control under those circumstances."

Quimby nodded. Finally, Devin had said something that made sense.

"You should know, sir, that from what I heard, your taking control kept the country from completely collapsing. If we don't undo what happened, you'll go down in history as one of our nation's greatest heroes."

As the general thought about what Devin said, there was a knock on the door. A housekeeper entered with a plate of sandwiches and two pitchers. When she'd left, Marcus started the video again and watched the whole recording for a second time while they ate.

When it completed, Devin asked, "Sir, do you have any questions? I'd like to get going. I'm eager to return to my time period."

"All the information I need is in here?" The general held up the pocket comp. "It has the location of the illegal lab, the names of those involved, and the date of the crisis. So I think you've completed your mission, Devin."

General Quimby stood and walked to Devin and shook his hand.

"Good luck, sir. I'm sure it isn't easy having this dropped on you. The fate of the world is literally in your hands."

Quimby got a grim look on his face and nodded. "I'll take care of this."

Devin left the study and headed outside. He nodded at the second agent as he left, but didn't see Warren Black as he departed. He took his pocket comp out and used it to summon a car. He instructed it to meet him in five minutes in the parking lot of the park where he had come through the portal. As he finalized the order, he got a warning on the comp. A request with only five minutes of lead time might not be able to be met, and the car might be up to ten minutes later than requested. He would have it take him to Matthew Becker's house. It would be late when he arrived, but he would feel better once he was that much closer to getting back to his time period.

He could've had the car pick him up at the general's house, but for some reason he was compelled to make sure no one would be tracking him.

Chapter Forty

GENERAL QUIMBY SAT LOOKING AT ALL THE DATA THE MAN had delivered from the future. The disaster was unbelievable. Billions dead, and it would happen in a couple months. That he had to stop it was indeed a pressure he'd never felt before.

The general went to his computer and started looking up information on Argon Technologies. He wanted to know more about who they were and who was funding their activities.

He heard a knock on the door, and Agent Warren Black stepped in.

"Sir, I found something you should be aware of."

"What is it?"

"When I left Devin here with you, I decided to do a little investigating. The security cameras caught a good picture of his face. I ran it through all databases and didn't find anything. No matter where he's from, he should be in there somewhere."

"And you found nothing?"

Quimby thought it might be because Devin came from the future. But only three years in the future. He should still look the same and be locatable by facial recognition.

"Not at first. I then started expanding the search wider

and wider. Eventually, I found a Devin Baker whose photo is a perfect match. The problem is that the photo was taken over 80 years ago, and that Devin Baker died as an old man twenty-three years ago. But the photo is a perfect match. There's more. When we admitted him, the security system queried his biochip and identified him as being Matthew Becker. I looked him up, and they're clearly not the same person. Devin isn't Matthew Becker, but he's using his biochip."

"So we have a man from the past delivering me a message from the future?" Quimby wondered aloud.

"Sir, I don't follow."

"No, you missed most of it. Is Devin still here?" The general hopped up from the desk, the pocket comp still held in his hand.

"He just left. He was on foot."

Quimby rushed for the door. He wanted more information from this Devin Baker. He yanked the door open, hurried toward the outside stairs and looked up and down the street for Devin. When the general's left foot went down the on the first step, the flat bottom of the slipper made contact with the rain covered, polished stone and shot out from under him. When the general landed, the back of his neck struck the edge of the first step, fracturing the second and third cervical vertebra. The momentum from his rapid movement out the door kept the body moving forward, and it tumbled down the eight stairs. As it fell, the head moved in many directions, and there was no support now that the bones at C2-C3 were fractured. by the time he came to rest on the sidewalk, his spinal cord at the site of the fracture was severed. There were also many small lacerations on the body, among which were several on the hand that had been holding the now-smashed pocket comp.

Warren Black gasped as the man he was tasked to protect, who had become a friend, took the horrendous fall.

He pressed the device on his collar. "Code 2, Code 2! The MQ is down. Start EMS now!" He raced down the stairs, to the general's side. He was terrified as to how bad it would be.

"General! General Quimby, can you hear me." Agent Black yelled as he knelt down, but there was no response.

The security team and EMS would do everything possible to save Marcus Quimby's life, but their efforts were all in vain. The only hope he had was a man who was standing in the parking lot of a nearby park, waiting for a car and listening to the sirens, oblivious to what had just happened.

Chapter Forty-One

THE HEADLIGHTS CAME DOWN THE ROAD AND ILLUMINATED THE parking lot as the robocar turned into it. Devin stepped forward to meet it, aware of more sirens on the outside of the park. He removed the rain poncho and shook it out as the vehicle stopped in front of him, and the rear door opened.

"I'm here for Doctor Matthew Becker," said a voice from inside the car.

"I'm Doctor Matthew Becker." Devin got into the car.

The door shut, and the vehicle turned to leave the park.

"Doctor Becker, are we still headed to your home address?" The Virtual Attendant asked. It had already queried the BioChip in Devin's arm and confirmed the address and payment method on file.

"Yes."

"We will arrive in about forty minutes. Would you like to listen to news, sports, or music on the way?"

"Relaxing music, volume low." Devin was amazed at how this car was doing everything without human involvement.

For several minutes, he watched as the vehicle got itself on the highway and accelerated. Eventually, he leaned back and closed his eyes as they traveled. Thinking about what had happened and how well it had gone, he smiled, feeling good. A bit damp from the rain, but still good.

He'd just done his part to save the world. It was now up to General Quimby. Devin didn't doubt that the general would handle this effectively. That man had taken the reigns of a nation in crisis and steered it back from the brink of collapse. Shutting down a research laboratory that was operating outside the law would be no problem for him.

Thirty-eight minutes later, Devin heard, "Doctor Becker. We will be arriving in one minute."

"Thank you." Then Devin wondered if it was normal in this time period to thank a car.

The vehicle stopped in a subdivision, directly in front of a ranch-style home. Devin took the pocket comp out and looked at the address info. After the door opened, and the virtual attendant wished him a good night, he exited without talking to the robotic car. As he walked towards the front door, he pulled up another video.

As he was getting ready to knock, he heard a clicking sound as the door unlocked and swung open. Hesitantly, Devin entered the house, realizing a sensor had read his biochip and had opened the door, assuming that he was the homeowner. He closed the door and wasn't sure what to do now that he was inside. Matthew and his family were probably all in bed. After taking a moment to think, Devin called out, "Hello!" He waited for several seconds and called out again, "Hello, Matthew!"

This time he heard something. Someone approached, still hidden in the darkness of the home. Devin turned toward the sound of the footsteps, with the pocket comp ready, and was startled to see a large black and brown Shepherd-Lab mix come around the corner. The dog was well in excess of a hundred pounds, and powerful looking. Devin wasn't concerned about it injuring him, but he didn't want Matthew's first sight of him to be that of him grappling with his dog.

The animal came right up to him, tail wagging. Devin realized this dog might be useful for deterring someone from breaking in, but would be useless once a burglar got inside.

Devin dropped to one knee, and when Matthew finally turned on a light and entered the room carrying a wooden baseball bat, Devin and the dog were already friends.

"Who are you and why are you in my house?"

Devin rose from the floor and the dog backed away, sensing his master's concern.

Devin found himself on the defensive end of the conversation. The encounter with the dog had cost him his plan to be assertive and take control.

"Matthew, I mean no harm," Devin said in his most friendly voice. "Watch this."

He held the pocket comp in front of Matthew's face, and the video played.

Matthew didn't reach for the device, but his eyes grew wide when he saw himself on the screen.

"We finally did it. We moved a person back in time. Devin here will show you all the information. I need you to listen to him. The whole situation is quite a bit different than we ever planned."

"Come in, Devin, and take a seat in the living room. I need to let my wife, Mallory, know what's going on. We were concerned that you were an intruder." As he said this, he held up the bat and smiled at Devin as he left the room to put it away.

When Matthew returned, he sat across from Devin. "So what's going on? I'm excited to hear we finally got the bugs worked out. But why are you here so late at night?"

Devin handed Matthew the pocket comp. "There's lots of information, videos, and all the technical data to advance your project to where it will be when I moved through time. However, I think it would be best if we started with me telling you the whole story, as I know it.

Chapter Forty-Two

DEVIN SLEPT SOUNDLY IN THE BECKER FAMILY'S GUEST ROOM and was awakened by someone shaking his arm and calling his name.

"Devin, you need to wake up," Matthew said.

Slowly, Devin started to awaken. He felt disoriented as to his location. Looking out the window, he saw that it was early. The sun was starting to rise. Then he focused on Matthew's face and things started to come back to him.

"Come on, Devin, get up!"

"What's wrong?" Devin asked. The anxiety in Matthew's voice registering with him.

"We have a big problem. Marcus Quimby is dead."

Devin leaped from the bed. "What happened? He can't be dead! He's still alive three years from now. I met him."

Matthew handed a pocket comp to Devin and triggered an online news broadcast.

"Authorities are reporting that General Marcus Quimby, the Chairman of the Joint Chiefs, is dead. He died at his home following some kind of an accident in front of his house at about 11:00 p.m. last night. The Federal Protective Service is looking for someone that may have information regarding the incident." Devin's photo appeared on the

screen. *"This man, who's either know as Devin Baker or Matthew Becker, may have information, and authorities are anxious to speak to him."*

Devin handed the device back to Matthew and with a quiver in his voice, "I left his house at about eleven. He was sitting in his study, reading the data I gave him. He's the only one with the information needed to stop the pandemic."

"If Quimby was alive three years from now, and is now dead, something you did must have changed the timeline."

"When I left, he was reading. I didn't do anything else."

"Well, they have my name. Probably from the biochip you have. It won't be long before the authorities come here. They'll be looking for information."

"I need to leave. I have to figure out what to do. You have the information needed to advance your and Brian's work. Once I get this figured out, I'll be in touch." Devin pulled out his pocket comp and requested a car.

"It looks like there are two options. Either you find someone else who can help you, or you stop the disaster yourself."

Devin paced the room, nervous energy needing release while studying information on his pocket comp. This continued for serval minutes until a gray car pulled up to the curb.

Matthew left the room, then returned and handed Devin something that looked like an elastic band.

"You might want this. It will hide the signal from the biochip. You can put it on and take it off as needed. Copying or altering a biochip is illegal. Hiding one is not."

Devin gave him a questioning look.

"I might have used it a few times in college." Matthew grinned.

"I will contact you." Devin took the band and hefted his backpack.

He left the house without looking back, and as Devin approached the car, the door opened.

"Good evening, Doctor Becker," the car said.

Devin took a seat in the back and the door closed.

"Doctor Becker, your car request didn't contain a destination."

"Take me to Pershing Park in Washington DC."

The vehicle began moving. "With nighttime traffic, we should arrive in approximately thirty-nine minutes."

Pershing Park is a 1.75-acre park named after General John Pershing. General Pershing served as commander of the American Expeditionary Force in Europe during World War I. The park serves as a memorial to that war. Located between 14th and 15th streets, the park is along Pennsylvania Avenue and a short walk from the White House. Devin thought that asking to be taken directly to the White House might raise some kind of alarm. He assumed it was just a matter of time before someone tracked the biochip, so he wanted to stay ahead of them. He needed to try to keep the focus on the information about the pandemic and not on the general's death. Also, the lower on the food chain he started, the harder it would be to fight his way up to the top.

They continued for what felt like half an hour. The car maneuvered to the right lane and began slowing to take an exit. That's when Devin noticed a red light blinking on the dashboard for a few seconds and then stop. The car's speed increased.

"What's happening?"

"Doctor Becker, I've been instructed to deliver you to an alternate location."

Chapter Forty-Three

DEVIN CONSIDERED WHAT WAS HAPPENING FOR ONLY A COUPLE seconds, then he forced his door open against the airflow at seventy miles per hour. He clutched his bag and threw himself out of the still accelerating car, gripping the back of his head so that his arms protected the skull, with the bag pressed into his face. He needed to survive the accident, even for just a few seconds. He slammed against the ground with extreme force. It happened so fast he couldn't be sure of everything that he injured. He felt something in his right shoulder break, and then as he tumbled across the asphalt, his hip and pelvis had something catastrophic happen. He also felt his left leg bending in a way that it was never intended to.

When he came to rest, he knew that there were many other injuries because the pain was everywhere and his breathing labored. He tried to scream but couldn't get a deep enough breath. He lay still, unable to move and feeling consciousness fading. Then a familiar sensation took over as his level of alertness snapped back. He was relieved when the intense pain suddenly vanished. He felt his bones and muscles moving back into place and healing. The next thing he became aware of was the wheels of a truck narrowly missing him as he lay on the side of the highway. He jumped to his feet and sprinted for the exit ramp. Only twenty seconds earlier, he'd still been in the car.

When Devin reached the bottom of the ramp, he moved into the shadows. Reached into his pocket and found the band that Matthew had given him, and started to slide it over his arm when he saw all the blood on his skin. His injuries, from diving out of the moving car, had existed for only a brief time, but it was enough for quite a bit of blood to come out, and it covered much of him. He noticed that his shirt was stained and torn apart. He removed it and took a water bottle from his pack. He used the cleanest parts of the wrecked shirt and some water to remove as much blood as he could from his skin. He checked and saw that his jeans had held up much better. There was blood on them, but he wasn't concerned about that. He took a spare shirt from the pack, put it on, and then placed the band over the biochip. Remembering the remaining pocket comps, he rechecked the bag and was relieved to see that the rugged cases had held up in the violent impact.

As Devin finished cleaning himself, he heard sirens approaching and jogged away from the highway ramp. His research, while pacing in Matthew's living room, had told him about Pershing Park. It would have been an excellent destination for him because it sat so close to the White House. Now, he assumed that there would soon be people waiting in the park for him. They would have gotten his intended destination from the RoboCar.

He moved several blocks over, walked about six miles, and approached the White House from the opposite direction. The long walk was an inconvenience, but the time allowed him to create the beginnings of a plan.

With the dramatic improvement in scanning technology,

White House security had significantly changed in the 2060s. Many of the fortress-like defenses were modified or removed, and advanced technology provided early warnings of possible threats. If Devin had been carrying any explosives, even bullets containing simple gunpowder, sensors would have activated. Then security would have intercepted him when he was still over a mile away. Because of this, other than the iconic fence that still surrounded the property, most of the physical barriers had been removed. Therefore, he was able to walk directly up to a small gatehouse that controlled access to a drive, which was used for deliveries to the Presidential Mansion.

The security guard looked up and saw Devin approaching, still fifty yards away. His shift had just started, and he was already having to deal with this. Here we go again, he thought. The posted signs were large, and their meaning clear. This route was for delivery traffic only. No walk-ups.

The guard then noticed the backpack, which were always a concern. He looked at his scanner again and made a few adjustments. There were no explosives and nothing metal large enough to be a weapon. There were two electronic devices that were identified as pocket comps. That was a bit strange, but not concerning. There were also three bottles of an unknown liquid. Scans gave an 88 percent chance that it was only water. Whatever it was, it wasn't explosive or flammable.

The more significant concern, the system said, was that there was no biochip responding. There were some people that refused them, but they were few and far between. More likely, he was hiding it. The security guard adjusted the sophisticated scanner and focused on the person's forearm. He now detected a faint signal, not enough to get any information, but there was a shielded biochip.

The man was now only about fifty feet away. There were stains and a few rips on his pants. The scanner indicated a 92 percent chance the stains were blood. As advanced as the portable scanner was, it couldn't determine if the blood was his, or even if it came from a human. He would need more sophisticated equipment for that.

"Sir, this entry is for vehicle traffic only! You've passed four signs informing you of that."

Devin continued to approach.

"Sir, please turn around and go back the way you came!" The guard yelled.

Devin walked up to the man who wore a short-sleeved white uniform shirt. The patch on his arm identified him as working for the Federal Protection Service. His nametag read *Chad James.*

"Officer James," Devin said in his most friendly voice. I apologize for my inappropriate approach and my disheveled appearance, but it was necessary. I need to speak to your supervisor immediately. There's a problem that I need to discuss with him or her."

"What kind of problem? Why are you shielding your biochip?"

"I'm sorry, but I'll explain all that to your supervisor."

"What is your name?"

"Devin Baker."

The guard developed a look of confusion. The name seemed familiar, but he couldn't place where he'd heard it before.

"Mr. Baker. I need you to uncover your biochip, then turn around and leave. This entrance is for vehicle traffic only. If you don't leave now, I'll summon others who'll place you under arrest."

Devin raised his left arm with his palm facing the guard. The palm split wide open, muscle and bone visible. As fast as it had appeared, the gruesome laceration disappeared, and he lowered his hand.

"Chad," Devin said forcefully. "get your supervisor now!"

With eyes wide, Chad tapped a hidden spot on his collar and began speaking. Devin couldn't hear all that he said, but he could see the bewilderment on Chad's face. He suppressed a grin. So far, things were going as planned.

Devin waited for about four minutes. The guard glanced at him occasionally, but didn't say anything more. Devin heard a noise and turned to see three people approaching. They were marching down the road, coming from the direction of the Presidential Mansion. Two were uniformed guards like Chad. One male, and the other female. The other was a male wearing a suit. The guards had holstered weapons that looked large and strange to Devin. The man in the suit walked in front. He also had a weapon of some kind concealed under his suit coat.

As he approached, he looked Devin over, and his expression indicated that he wasn't impressed.

The man in the suit spoke. "I understand that you're insisting on speaking with a supervisor with the Federal Protective Service and that you caused some kind of disturbance here."

"Yes, I need to speak to someone in charge. But I've made no disturbance, sir. I'm no threat."

The man looked at Chad and pointed to the scanner.

"All clear," Chad said.

"The supervisor of the Federal Protection Service isn't available at this time. I'm with the Secret Service. You need to leave immediately."

Devin stepped forward and held out his hand. "My name is Devin, and we need to talk. There's a problem that I need to discuss with the President. I'd be happy to start with his Chief of Staff or whoever is in charge of his protective detail."

The agent ignored the offered hand, closed his eyes for a second, and sighed in frustration. Another nut who thought he could get access to the President. This is precisely why the Federal Protective Service was on the job here—to keep the Secret Service from having to deal with this nonsense. Today, of all days, the FPS supervisor called in sick and her replacement was still thirty minutes away.

"People don't just walk up and see the President. Now, these two officers will escort you off the grounds. If you cause any problems or return, you'll be arrested."

The two officers who had arrived with the agent stepped forward and each took one of Devin's arms. As they tried to escort him away, they dropped to their knees and began screaming. The flesh on their forearms had burst open almost as soon as they touched him. They immediately release him. Devin held his hands open, fingers spread at his chest level. He looked at Chad and the Secret Service agent, both of which now held odd-looking weapons in their hands.

"I mean no harm. I can help them." Devin turned to the woman on the ground, holding her mangled arm.

As he bent down, a sensation that felt like being burned and electrocuted at the same time pounded into him and knocked him to his knees. The pain rapidly disappeared.

"Stop that foolishness," Devin said, forcing a calm tone, and gave the agent the look one would use when correcting a young child.

Devin grabbed the hand of the woman on the ground and restored her arm to normal. He then stood and helped her to her feet. He then went and held out his hand to the second guard. By the time Devin had helped him to his feet, his wounds were gone.

He approached the agent. "Put the weapon away."

"How did you do that? This thing is guaranteed to drop a charging rhino and keep it down for ten minutes." The agent indicated the weapon as he holstered it.

"Do I look like a rhino?" Devin fought a grin. "Let's go.

Head of Secret Service or Chief of Staff. Your choice." He started walking past the guard gate and followed the path that the agent and guards had taken on their way to the gatehouse. "Come on, guys. I mean no threat. If I wanted to cause problems, I'd be inside already."

Chapter Forty-Four

THE SECRET SERVICE AGENT STAYED A SHORT DISTANCE BEHIND Devin and spoke to someone inside via a hidden radio. Devin couldn't hear what they said, but he could tell that he was letting others on his team know of the situation. As they approached the White House, the agent had caught up to Devin.

"So I told you my name," Devin said. "You never told me yours."

"Travis. Travis Marks."

"Nice to meet you, Travis. Please don't shoot me with your ray gun again. It was kinda painful."

"I realized why your name is familiar," Agent Marks said, ignoring Devin's other comment, "you're the one they're looking for in connection to General Quimby's death. Correct?"

"They want to ask me some questions. I didn't directly have anything to do with the general's death. I'd left before it happened. His death is why I had to come here. In a way, he was a friend, and his death is quite troubling to me. However, that's insignificant compared to what I need to discuss with the President."

"You do know that I'm not taking you to see the President? I couldn't, even if I wanted to."

"Of course. I don't need you, too. You are getting me into the building and in touch with those above you. That's your role in this. They will get me to the President when I show and explain to them what I have. I assure you, I mean absolutely no harm."

Agent Marks thought about this. He realized Devin was manipulating the whole situation, and started to doubt the decision to take him inside. It was beginning to look like this was part of a bigger plan.

"This way, Devin." Agent Marks directed Devin away from the main path and towards a smaller door.

Devin followed.

Agent Marks approached the door and it clicked open as it detected his BioChip. They entered the building and there were two additional agents waiting inside for them. They fell into line behind Devin as they walked down a hall. They passed through two more doors and came across a large rectangular scanner built into the walls and ceiling of the hallway.

"Devin, we will need you to walk through the scanner in just a minute." Agent Marks passed through, then went to a console and activated the powerful scanner. "OK, walk through it."

Devin froze, a little concerned. "Will this scanner harm electronics or the data stored on them?"

"No, it's perfectly safe."

Devin nodded, walked through and continued up to the console, where he looked at the holographic display. He could see all the contents of the backpack and another image of his body.

"If it makes you more comfortable, I'll leave the backpack here. I just need the pocket comps."

"No, you can keep it. We see what everything is. There are no concerns."

Agent Marks shut the scanner off, and they continued down the hall and into an area marked as *Security Holding*. The first room they passed had sparse furnishings, with just a table and three chairs. They entered the second room. It had some decorations, a couch, and a few comfortable-looking chairs. Devin sat in a padded blue chair, and the three agents entered the room, leaving the door open.

"Someone will be here in a few minutes," said Agent Marks.

"No problem." Devin opened the pack and removed a bottle of water and a package of the food he'd brought from the future.

One of the other agents said "What is that you're eating?"

"I'm not exactly sure. It's very dry and has no taste."

"Then why are you eating it?"

"I wasn't able to bring anything that contained plant or animal material in it. This is what they gave me."

The three agents looked at one another, confused.

"Devin, I can order you a sandwich if you want," Agent Marks said.

"Thank you. I haven't had anything other than these wafers in the last fourteen hours, and I'm hungry."

The agent who had inquired about Devin's food stepped out of the room to place the order.

While they were waiting, another man in a suit stepped into the room. He looked older, with graying hair.

"Devin, I'm Douglas Miller, the supervisory agent on duty. I understand you have something to tell me and that there have been some unusual things going on here since you arrived."

"Yes, sir, I do. I apologize for the disruption I caused, but I need to talk to the President and I don't have much time. So I've used a bit of drama to get your people's attention."

"I see. You certainly have our attention. What's the critical information?"

"First, sir, please go online and look up Devin Baker in the early 2020s."

"That would have been about eighty-five years ago?"

"Correct." Agent Miller entered the information in the console. "I don't see what that could have to do with…" He looked at Devin and then back the holographic image hovering in the air in front of him. "Travis, look at this."

Travis moved behind his boss and looked at the image.

"No doubt you've captured dozens of images of me," Devin said, "starting before I even made it to the gatehouse. Even in my time, there's facial recognition capability. What does your system say?"

The men didn't respond. They spoke in whisperers and continued to work at the console. Every so often, they would look up at Devin with confused expressions.

Devin sat quietly, except for when someone brought in his food. They had given him a turkey sandwich on wheat bread, with lettuce and tomato. There were some pita chips and a glass of lemonade as well. Devin scarfed down the food and finished before the two agents had completed their research. Devin could hear only a little of what the agents said, but at one point, he heard Travis say, "This isn't possible."

Eventually, the two moved away from the console, looking at Devin.

"Devin, the facial comparison says there's a perfect match between the images from eighty-five years ago and what we captured today," said Agent Miller.

"I know." Devin nodded.

"Also, the scanner that I had you walk through is extremely sophisticated and captured your DNA sequence. Not only in your body, but also from the blood on your pants. We know that the blood on your pants is yours and only a few hours old, but also there are no injuries that the blood could have come from. We compared the DNA to a sample that was taken about seventy years ago from that Devin Baker, and you're a perfect match."

Devin nodded. "That's what I'd have expected, though I didn't know your scanner would be able to capture my DNA. That's impressive."

"I forwarded the data to our tech team. They're looking into it a little more deeply. I remember hearing about the Devin Baker from sixty to eighty years ago and the things he could do. Exactly the kind of things our people are reporting that they saw you do. Can you explain any of this please?"

"One last thing I need to show you first. Am I correct that a biochip stores a record of its activity?"

"That is correct."

Devin pulled down the band that blocked his biochip. "It isn't mine. It's cloned. I needed to be able to operate here, but I didn't have one. Check the activity on it and the dates it was queried."

While returning to the console to scan the chip, Miller said. "You didn't have a biochip of your own because you're from the past. That's what you're saying. Correct?"

"Yes, that's true. I'm the same Devin from eighty-five years ago, but that's only a part of it."

The two agents again looked at the holographic data that scrolled in front of their faces. And yet again they looked at one another, still confused.

"Devin, I was starting to believe what we were seeing," Agent Miller said. "Now I'm confused again. It looks like you're from eighty-five years in the past and wearing a biochip that was recently implanted and tested three years from now, in the future."

"If you guys think that's confusing. You should be on this side of it. Two days ago, I was minding my own business in the year 2023 and had no idea time travel would ever exist."

Devin dug into the backpack, finally satisfied that they

would take him seriously. He removed the pocket comp, identical to the one he'd given General Quimby before his death.

"This comp is locked to my cloned biochip and General Quimby's. I've unlocked three videos. Please take them to the President and make sure she sees them immediately. There isn't much time. I was sent here from three years in the future, by General Quimby to give the General Quimby from your time this information so a global pandemic could be avoided. After I gave it to him, something happened and he was killed. But I knew him three years from now. My interaction with him must have triggered whatever accident killed him. After that happened, I had to come up with a new plan. That's why I'm here."

Chapter Forty-Five

THE FOUR HELICOPTERS STREAKED ACROSS THE ARIZONA desert. General Dwain Peck, Director of the U.S. Army Medical Research Institute of Infectious Diseases (USAM-RID), rode aboard the first. He looked up and noted that the dozen heavily armed special operations soldiers were sitting quietly, mentally preparing themselves for whatever they might experience on the ground. Dr. Jake Dexter of Argon Technologies accompanied them.

Dr. Dexter had been summoned to the Pentagon two days ago, supposedly to report on the progress of the work Argon Technologies was conducting. Following his report, he was immediately arrested and questioned at length about the research his company was doing. Other arrests within the Pentagon were carried out. Military police apprehended all those involved in the ordering and funding of the illegal projects.

During his questioning, Dr. Dexter had confirmed that there was a power shutdown of non-essential systems sched-uled in two weeks.

General Peck thought back to when he had received the briefing on this situation. Most of it was presented by a young man who was obviously a little out of place at the White House. No one provided the man's last name, title, or position. They just called him Devin. The President had even differed to him a couple of times when questions were raised. Apparently he was the source of information about the extreme danger at the Argon lab.

The general had received lots of data to read, but they told him nothing about who the young man was or where the information had originated. The documents were noticeably incomplete, with specific information having been redacted. But while his information was incomplete, Peck's mission was clear. He had to, at all costs, secure every sample of a developmental bioweapon known as X-5207, and all data pertaining to it. He also need to confiscate the thousand doses of a vaccine against this bioweapon.

While in the air, Dr. Dexter had contacted the head of security for Argon Technologies. He informed General Peck that several U.S. military helicopters were on the way and that the security team shouldn't get in the way. Argon security would continue to handle the outside security posts, and the Army personnel would be taking charge inside.

The first two helicopters landed together and their teams quickly disembarked. The helicopters needed to get back off the ground and make room for the other two, which were hovering nearby. In the second aircraft were twelve men and women in one-piece tight-fitting jumpsuits, and two men in business suits. The group in jumpsuits waited for the equipment which would be coming in on the last two aircraft. The men in suits were FBI agents. While the remainder of the team unloaded their equipment, the rest of the new arrivals descended into the laboratory complex.

Dr. Dexter knew his orders. He was to make sure that no one sounded an alarm or destroyed any evidence. If he cooperated, when charges were filed he would receive special consideration.

"I need everyone to meet in conference room one," Jake Dexter announced to everyone in the office area, then activated the internal communication system which would broadcast his voice through the entire facility. "Everyone not in the containment area needs to assemble in CR-one immediately."

When the first Argon employees approached the conference room, they stared wide-eyed at the heavily armed special operations commandos standing in the halls and at each doorway. As everyone moved to the conference room, the last of the newcomers entered the facility. There were six of them wearing state-of-the-art containment suits. They were fully encapsulated and had their own air supply. Three of them were carrying energy weapons that had been specially modified to be usable with the containment suits. These teams headed straight to the first hatch leading into the lab.

Dr. Elizabeth Cox didn't know what was happening. She heard the announcement for everyone to assemble. However, she was in the hot zone and couldn't easily remove herself to see what was going on. She knew that the work they were doing wasn't exactly legal, but she'd put four years of her life into this project and was excited about how far they'd come. She couldn't imagine anyone stopping this work after there had been so much progress.

When the airlock opened and the four people entered, Dr. Cox palmed the small glass vial in her gloved hand.

One of the armed people said, "I'm Major Anderson with USAMRID. I need everyone to secure any samples that you're working with and proceed to decontamination. We will explain everything once everyone is fully decontaminated and in conference room one." His voice sounded surprisingly clear through the mask.

Dr. Cox obediently exited the hot zone and proceeded through the three stages of decontamination. As she moved along, she kept the vial trapped between her thumb and palm. After showering, she dressed and slipped the vial into her pocket. She then froze and looked around. She was concerned that someone might have spotted the move, but no one reacted, so she went to the final airlock, and when she stepped out, she saw the strangest sight. There stood Peggy Wilson, a lab tech. She was crying and had her hands bound behind her back. Two men with visible credentials reading *FBI* were escorting her out of the conference room.

Dr. Cox overheard the female agent say, "We need to know all the details about what you've been doing."

Elizabeth heard just a fragment of the conversation, but it was enough to give her hope that maybe she was wrong, and this had nothing to do with the work on X-5207.

Her hand brushed her leg and she felt the vial in her pocket. Tonight, this would be in her refrigerator at home. She wasn't taking any chances that someone might try to stop her research.

Epilogue

YEAR 2024

DEVIN WALKED ACROSS A STREET IN THE CITY OF DHAMAR, IN Yemen. He needed to stretch his legs after being cooped up in the hospital for the last six hours. He'd been cautioned not to wander around since the area was known for violence. All morning long, he'd heard gunshots around the hospital. Already he'd helped three additional people that had been brought in with gunshot wounds.

As he strolled along, he passed several buildings that were just bombed-out shells. In one case, he wasn't sure what was keeping the remains of a government building from falling. There were occasional cars driving down the street, and burned-out abandoned vehicles on the side of the road. Cleaning up the debris was apparently not a high priority.

Devin's mind wandered to the man he thought of as the greatest person he'd ever met—General Marcus Quimby. He had unified and saved the nation from destruction. Unfortunately, no one else would ever think of him that way, because in the version of history that remained, that never happened. People would remember him as a U.S. Army general and the Chairman of the Joint Chiefs who slipped and died on a rain-soaked step, in his slippers.

It had been just over six months since Devin had been returned to his own time. Matthew Becker had gotten his time travel process advanced enough, and freed Devin from the future that had trapped him. Things hadn't gone well for Devin since returning. He'd considered returning to holding the large events, but it didn't feel right. He'd always conducted those with the belief that he was using a divine gift. Now that he knew the truth, he felt like a fraud. He'd been helping people, so he was still doing good work. But he couldn't bring himself to stand on a big stage with his name in giant gold letters anymore.

His thoughts went back to what General Quimby had said to him. He still had a purpose—an alternate purpose. But what would he do now that the purpose he was created for was complete?

At times like this, when he was deep in thought, he found himself pressing a finger into the flesh of his right forearm, feeling the faint shape of the biochip still with him. He'd considered having Brian remove it before they sent him back. But in the end, he decided to keep the futuristic technology. That, and the last pocket comp. He knew he should have left it in the future, but he decided to bring home with him. Its battery had died a week ago, and he had no way to charge it. However, it served as a reminder of what would have happened, if he hadn't prevented the disaster

After a week of sitting around contemplating the purpose of his life, the director of the Federal Emergency Management Agency (FEMA) contacted him. Like almost everyone else, FEMA leadership knew about the things he could do. They wanted to offer him a job. He would do contract work for them. In the event of a disaster anywhere in the U.S., he would travel onsite to assist those who were critically injured. The pay wasn't impressive, and he would only receive payment when he was at a disaster site, but the idea intrigued him. He told them he would think about it.

After three days, he returned to them with a counteroffer. He agreed to a one-year contract. His salary would now be much better, and he would split his time between FEMA, the U.S. military, and the UN. It was up to those three agencies to figure out how to make the numbers work.

He would be available for FEMA as they suggested, but he would also travel to areas where the U.S. military was deployed. He would help U.S. Forces by healing any service personnel that were injured. If neither of those agencies had an immediate need, the UN could send him to any place on the planet to use his abilities in times of crisis.

He had a high-speed aircraft at his disposal and could be at the scene of an event anywhere on the planet in less than a day. Because of that, he was here in Yemen, at the sight of a bombing in a market square the day prior. Many of those injured in the bombing had been children, and Devin had spent all morning healing the survivors.

He walked a little further and then decided to head back. There were some less critical patients in the hospital that he hadn't visited with yet. He wanted to see as many of them as possible before his flight left in three hours. Unlike in the U.S., these underfunded hospitals which survived on donations were glad to have him come in and reduce their occupancy.

As he turned to go back to the hospital, something knocked him to the ground, and severe pain shot up his arm. There didn't seem to be anyone close by, and he assumed it had been a bullet that was intended for another target.

He got to his feet and casually headed back to the hospital while examining the bloody hole in the shoulder of his shirt, the pain now gone. He moved the arm in all directions. No problems.

As Devin entered the building, he walked past the armed guards, who stared wide-eyed at the bullet hole in his shirt with the fresh blood around it. He went to the staircase and headed to the second floor. There remained one hall that he hadn't visited.

The first room and saw a standard six-person room. Two of the beds were empty. Since Devin's arrival, hospital occupancy had dropped significantly and patients were being moved around to make things less crowded. The man in the third bed was asleep, but the forth was wide awake and looking at him. Devin was taken aback to see that the man wasn't Arabic.

"You Devin Baker?" the man said, with an Australian accent.

"Yes, I am." Devin answered as he grabbed a straight-back chair and pulled it up next to the bed, and could see that the man's leg was bandaged and immobilized.

"I had hoped you'd stop in. I'm Danny Cooper. I'm with Doctors Without Borders."

"Then why are you playing patient?" Devin asked with a smile.

Danny smiled back. "This sad place can't keep their own staff, so I was sent in to help them out. On my third day here, I was shopping in the market, along the side of the road, and some nut job hits me with his car. The gal I was with says it looked like he did it on purpose. I'm not sure. Either way, he didn't stop and my femur was broken. An open fracture. Bone sticking right out. I've seen it dozens of times, but to have it happen to you is another thing. After the surgery, I ended up with an infection, and it's just now starting to get better."

"I'm sorry. I hadn't heard about you, or I'd have stopped in sooner."

"Things got rather hectic with the bombing. I've been here listening to all that's going on. It's tough to be the cause of more work for the others instead of being the one doing the work" Danny said.

"Well, Danny, are you ready to get out of that bed?" Devin asked as he held out his hand.

Danny took the outstretched hand and Devin felt the sensation of something leaving him and immediately being replaced. He smiled when he saw Danny's eyes get wide. A few seconds later, Devin, guided by Danny, removed the leg immobilizer and the bandages.

"This really is amazing! Thank you." Danny stood and walked around the room, then after a minute, returned and sat on the side of the bed. "Do you mind me asking you a question, Devin?"

"Not at all." Devin retook his seat.

"Why the big change? I heard about your big shows. Hundreds of people healed each night. You were making great money."

"I guess I had a change of conscience. Something happened that shook me up a bit. It made me question my motivations. You might say I'm re-evaluating my decisions. The shows were beneficial, but the huge productions and the glamor now seem kind of over the top. The new me wants to be more personal. My priorities are different."

Danny nodded, thinking that he understood. "Sounds like you want to move from the stage to the trenches."

Devin nodded "I signed a one year contract. We'll see how it goes. I'm not sure where I'll finally end up. I'm not saying there won't ever be the big events again—they do help many people. They would just probably be in a city park, not a concert hall."

"It sounds like the one thing you know is that you want to keep using this gift to help others."

Devin nodded. "I used to focus on the idea that God gave me this gift. Now that I've re-evaluated things, I realize we all have gifts, and it doesn't matter if we're born with them or if we've perfected them over time, God calls us to use those gifts for his glory. Now that I understand that, I have to figure out how I'm going to do it. The one thing I know is that it won't be on a stage with my name in giant gold letters."

As they sat together, thinking in silence, they could hear sirens approaching.

"Well, Doctor Danny Cooper, are you ready to get back to work?" Devin stood.

Danny also stood and looked down at his hospital gown. "I think I should find some pants first."

He put his arm over Devin's shoulder and the two of them walked into the hall.

Dear reader,

We hope you enjoyed reading *Alternate Purpose*. Please take a moment to leave a review, even if it's a short one. Your opinion is important to us.

Discover more books by Christopher Coates at

https://www.nextchapter.pub/authors/christopher-coates-science-fiction-author

Want to know when one of our books is free or discounted? Join the newsletter at

http://eepurl.com/bqqB3H

Best regards,

Christopher Coates and the Next Chapter Team

You might also like:
The Ark by Christopher Coates

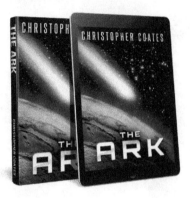

Click here to read the first chapter for free

Alternate Purpose
ISBN: 978-4-86745-884-6

Published by
Next Chapter
1-60-20 Minami-Otsuka
170-0005 Toshima-Ku, Tokyo
+818035793528

18th April 2021

CPSIA information can be obtained
at www.ICGtesting.com
Printed in the USA
BVHW032339270421
605943BV00009B/1118